MW00875457

The Prospector's Voyage

by

James Ballou

authorHOUSE

1663 Liberty Drive, Suite 200
Bloomington, Indiana 47403
(800) 839-8640
www.authorhouse.com

This book is a work of fiction. Places, events, and situations in this story are purely fictional and any resemblance to actual persons, living or dead, is coincidental.

© 2004 James Ballou
All Rights Reserved.

No part of this book may be reproduced, stored in a retrieval system, or transmitted by any means without the written permission of the author.

First published by AuthorHouse 08/03/04

ISBN: 1-4184-8454-7 (sc)

Printed in the United States of America
Bloomington, Indiana

This book is printed on acid-free paper.

CHAPTER I

Nathan Clayburn waited until he got to California to outfit himself. Twenty years earlier that likely wouldn't have been a sound plan, because prices charged for tools and supplies were often outrageously high during the height of the gold rush years in the Mother Lode country, and anyone traveling from afar would need a load of provisions just to get him there. Nathan was no more than a child in those days.

But in 1870, a man could ride the new railway system all the way from Omaha to Sacramento in less than five days. The same trip by wagon train could consume months, and it would be a hard journey.

Nathan boarded the train carrying a single shoulder bag. Besides a change of clothing, he had packed what few possessions he owned, which included his folding razor for shaving, block of soap, handkerchief, hair comb, a four-inch jackknife, the pocket watch and chain that his grandfather had given him, and the revolver he had paid ten silver dollars for to a veteran of the Civil War, who claimed to have used it to kill two Yankee soldiers. It was a five shot forty-four caliber caplock made by B.F. Joslyn. Included with the revolver was a small copper flask of gunpowder, a tiny can of caps, and two-dozen lead balls in a little buckskin pouch.

Nathan also carried with him his entire life's savings in gold and silver coins, which he planned to use to buy supplies for his expedition. He carried a shopping list that he had revised nearly half a dozen times already, trying to adjust it to his budget.

By far his most important possession, he believed however, was the map he had acquired of the Sierra Nevada Mountains, now neatly folded and protected in a linen sleeve within his bag. He had studied that square of parchment perhaps a hundred times, and by now had committed much of it to memory.

He had never before been west of the Missouri River. He boarded the train in Nebraska with visions of the western mountains; his head filled with the numerous stories he'd read and heard, and his dreams of finding a hidden wealth of gold out there somewhere. Inspired by tales of great fortunes reaped by prospectors and minors since 1849, he became obsessed with the possibility of doing the same, ignoring the more common accounts of gold hunters who'd gone bust trying. Nathan knew there was nothing short of dying that could prevent him from checking it out for himself.

He took a deep breath after he stepped off the train, inhaling the dry California air, and he looked around him, taking in the new scenery with a sense of enthusiasm more intoxicating than anything he'd felt up to now. He had planned this trip for several years, dreaming about it almost constantly, and now he had arrived. There would be traveling yet ahead of him to reach the gold fields he hoped to find, but he was in California now, and this was a dream come true.

Sacramento was a lot like he had imagined it, and it was a town with a look of permanence, still there and alive years after the initial boom of the 1850's.

Nathan saw himself as a man born for the West. Standing just one inch shy of six feet tall, and with a muscular build from half a dozen years of farm labor, usually accomplishing as much work as two average ranch hands or more, he believed he could do anything, and do it better than most. If ever there was anyone suited to the rigors of a wild land, it was Nathan Clayburn. Of that he was certain, as certain as he'd ever been about anything.

And he'd done a good bit of reading about California, about its history, and its geography, whenever he could ferret out such literature in the bigger city libraries. He was as ambitious a self-educator as he was a laborer, often to the bewilderment of his fellow ranch hands, who could see no useful purpose in book learnin'. And while a good many of them could be found in a tavern between jobs drinking away their wages, Nathan tended to hoard up his own earnings until he'd saved a nest egg sufficient to embark on his westward journey.

A follower of dreams was Nathan. Woven of the same fiber as men who found their way west before him, he left behind everything familiar to embrace the unknown, and he was hardly thwarted by the promises of danger. And like so many others who'd made the same journey, Nathan was not the sort to be dissuaded from the path he'd chosen.

And he left behind quite a lot, by the standards of most folks. An offer for a management position at a lumber mill came from the wealthy business owner, who happened to be the father of the young lady he courted for a time, Miss Elizabeth Dennison. But attaining such a life of prosperity by such means was not compatible with his own sense of dignity, and when he realized it, he also discovered that he did not particularly care to spend his life married to a woman so accustomed to privileged living, and so adverse to the struggles that shape human character.

It was not with much distress that he left her behind in Kansas City, after explaining his course, for he knew well enough that she would attract the affections of another man before long. That would not be difficult for a lady so perfectly attractive, and with so many lines cast her way from within her own social world. The focus of his attention, he explained to her, would be forever on those western mountains, and it was not within his power to ignore his overwhelming desire to visit them. Her inability to understand it only confirmed his verdict.

But now he was free from all of that. The life he left behind him was more than a thousand miles away, and that was fine by him. He could keep himself well centered here in his purpose without distraction, and the situation could only be considered ideal.

He decided to take a walk along the streets of Sacramento and familiarize himself with the town. It would be his home for a couple days while he made the final preparations for his expedition. And there was a lot to do. He would need to be outfitted with supplies, and determine what route to take. He would have a lot of questions to ask the locals who were familiar with the surrounding area. The more information he could collect, the better.

He stepped into a saloon for a drink. He wasn't much of a drinker, but there were always stories to be heard in saloons. Some of them might actually have useful information, if it could be sorted out from all the wild exaggerations and drunken fantasies one could almost always expect to hear in such a place.

He ordered a glass of whiskey, and asked the bartender about local prospecting. If anyone knew the stories folks told, it'd be the local bartender. That would hold true just about everywhere. And the man behind the counter in this case seemed perfectly willing to discuss the topic at length. It was a slow time of day in there, and he was probably bored with so few customers.

"Most of the bigger operations closed down five to ten years ago," he explained "and the best of the surface gold seems to'a been picked clean longer ago than that. Least, that's mostly true in this valley. Some still work the mountain streams. Ain't but a few mines still operatin' in them mountains. But ever so often ya hear about some monster of a nugget some lucky mortal turns up, like that one found outside Sierra City last year, but those are mighty rare anymore."

He set a glass in front of Nathan and poured a shot of whiskey. Noticing he had his full attention, he continued...

"There's an old timer livin' up in them mountains east of here, though, who's done mite well. Nobody knows where he finds 'em, but he's known to come into Sacramento with bright yellow nuggets you wouldn't believe. He's been in here a few times and had some drinks, but he ain't a big spender. And he don't talk much about anything. I saw one of them nuggets he sold. Mighty impressive. Heard it was thirty ounces."

"I don't suppose he's easy to find, if someone wanted to talk to him." Nathan inquired.

The bartender shook his head. "Lots of folks'd like to have a talk with him, all right. But he don't socialize much, and he don't like to talk about his gold."

Nathan downed the whiskey, and planted the empty glass on the counter in front of him. The bartender refilled the glass without asking him if he wanted another. Nathan never drank much, but in this case resigned himself to downing two glasses of whiskey if it kept the bartender talking. He would go slower on that second one.

"There've been some who've gone after him, tryin' to get his gold from him, but they were never seen around here again. I don't think he wants no trouble, but that don't keep folks away. He's a strange one – a bit suspicious of anyone and everyone.

"Story goes that he came out to California in 1850 with his family, huntin' gold, like most of us when we first come out here. Anyway, he was bushwacked and robbed by claim jumpers. It's rumored that he killed every last one of the bunch, and they say there was five of 'em in the group. But before he did, they so severely beat his wife and boy that they later died. His boy was just a toddler."

Nathan had raised his glass to drink, but stopped when he heard the part about the old timer's family being killed. He slowly lowered the full glass, setting it back down and then he took his hand off the glass.

"Well that's just awful." He said "That why he lives in the mountains, away from everyone?"

The bartender nodded "In the fight is where they say he lost his right eye. Whenever I've seen him, he's always wearing a patch over that eye, but it could be a wild tale just the same. Could've lost his eye any number of other ways."

"What's this old timer's name?" Nathan asked. His curiosity was roused, but he wasn't resigned entirely to accept the story as fact just yet.

The bartender thought on it for a moment, then shook his head. "Don't rightly know. I can picture the old codger sitting there having a drink, wearing that leather patch over his eye, not talkin' to no one, but can't say I ever heard anyone ever mention his name."

"Well, I need to find him and talk to him, if he knows where to find gold. That's what I came here for." Nathan stated, then swigged down half the contents of his second glass.

"It ain't advised." The bartender warned. "Like I said, he ain't particularly friendly, 'specially to those tryin' to get his gold. But that's your affair. I told you all I know about him."

"Not looking to take any gold from him. I don't want *his* gold. Just figure I could learn a thing or two from him, that's all." He finished his drink then stood up, reaching into his pocket and drawing his hand out with a few coins, which he tossed down next to the empty glass before the bartender filled it again.

"Obliged for the information, Mister." Nathan said, tipping his hat before turning to leave.

The bartender glanced down and noticed the coins reflecting sunlight from a window into his eyes. "Good luck to you, Sir." He said, looking up to see Nathan heading for the door.

It was getting late into the afternoon when Nathan walked into an inn that had a vacancy, and he reserved it for two nights. He expected to be able to acquire all of his needed supplies within that time frame. Sacramento, he told himself, should have stores to sell everything a man could ever need. The availability of equipment wasn't likely to be his biggest concern here. His limited resources would require some special planning, however, if he was going to properly outfit himself for such an expedition as he had planned. A man could always use more gear than he could afford, and good equipment was always expensive. But Nathan had saved his wages a long time. He wasn't rich by any means, but he had some money. He would make the best use of it.

It was an hour after sunrise the following morning when he was directed to a pasture with a selection of horses and mules for sale. He decided to make transportation his first priority, considering the miles he would be covering.

"You'll want a horse for riding, plus a couple mules or pack horses." The man recommended.

Nathan shook his head. "Don't plan to carry that many supplies right now. Might have as much as a hundred and fifty pounds on the outside, including tack and saddle, but not much more than that. Can't afford much more than that. Hope I won't be needing more this time of year. Now I weigh about one-seventy, so I figure an animal that can carry three-hundred pounds without too much trouble should work out just fine. Don't plan to push things too hard."

The man pointed toward a good-sized bay mule grazing near the far fence. "That one over there can pack four-hundred pounds and go as far as twenty miles a day with such a load, prob'ly better'n any animal I got for sale. He's a brute all right, but he's also fussy about who rides him, and who he works for. He was gelded early, so he's usually even tempered, so long as he likes ya. And he'll do damned near anything you ask him to, if he likes ya. But if he don't care for ya, he can be a real problem. I've known him to brace up and refuse to move at the worst of moments. I don't have the patience for that sort of thing. When he decides not to move, he won't budge even if he knows a steam engine's a rollin' towards him. My huntin' partner says just the opposite about him. It's all in whether he takes to ya or not."

"He and I are a lot alike, then." Nathan commented. "If I like the way he rides, we'll talk some business."

The man disappeared briefly into a barn and returned with an old beat up saddle, saddle blanket, and weathered bridle with a rusty bit, and handed it all to Nathan.

"Let's see how he takes to you, Sir. I'll let you do the honors."

Nathan took the tack from the man, and carried it over his shoulder as he entered the gate into the yard. He approached the mule casually from the side so as not to surprise him, talking to him in an easy confident tone the entire time. And while he spoke to the creature, he proceeded to saddle him up so naturally that he encountered no resistance, and once everything was properly adjusted and cinched, he eased himself up into the saddle and rode the gentle beast to the gate.

"Looks healthy enough." He said. "This one might do, if the price is reasonable."

The man had a surprised look on his face. "Tell ya what; ain't seen that animal cooperate that easy before with anyone, not even with my huntin' partner. I'll do you well on the price just to see him go with you. He's taken a shinin' to ya, all right. But where'd ya learn to handle animals like that?"

"We used plenty of mules and horses on the farms where I've worked. Learned not to fight with them. Get a lot more work done if you treat 'em decent. My grandfather taught me that."

"Your grand dad must've been a smart fella, if you learned all that from him."

"Smartest I've ever known." Nathan said.

After negotiating they settled on a price acceptable to both, and Nathan walked his new friend down a busy street, leading him by a simple rope halter he'd fashioned. He still had some gear to purchase, including the necessary tack and camp provisions, and he stopped in at a hardware store after picketing the mule just outside to the rail.

In the back of the store rested close to a dozen saddles on racks, and he searched for one that might well conform to the shape of a mule's back. The store was well stocked with fine new saddles, but most were well outside his price range. He finally settled on a simple used one that looked about right.

"You'll need a good rifle if you're fixin' to spend much time in the hills." The storekeeper advised, after Nathan indicated where he planned to travel. "And the Winchester repeater is beyond question the most popular."

Nathan liked the Winchester, and he'd examined one before in a store back in Missouri. He remembered that attractive brass receiver, and the convenient lever that cycled fresh cartridges into the chamber as fast as a man could work it. The Winchester could shoot a number of times before the shooter had to reload. It seemed as if everyone was always talking about it, and Nathan had been tempted to pony up for one on several occasions, but each time decided against it on account of the price. Maybe now it was time to buy one, he thought to himself, as the storekeeper handed it to him. Having allotted just so much for a long gun, he cast an offer substantially less than the retail price.

"Can't do it." The man said, retrieving the weapon back out of Nathan's hands. "Just that plenty others will buy the rifle, glad to get one at any price."

He then drew Nathan's attention to another rifle, picking it up out of the rack and handing it to him.

"The Ballard breech-loading single-shot is a cartridge gun, and in my opinion a very good product. It ain't as costly as the Winchester, but it's still a stretch handier than any front loader. And this'n shoots harder than the Winchester. Since I've had this piece in my store goin' on six months and it ain't yet sold, I'll make you a fair deal. Hell, I'll even toss in two boxes of cartridges if you want it. It shoots forty-six longs. They're bigger than the forty-fours those Winchesters and Henrys use. The forty-six is a rimfire cartridge, just like the forty-four, but it's got a longer case, and holds more powder."

It was just at the limit of what Nathan knew he could afford, but he also knew how important a good rifle could be in the wilds, and that Ballard looked like a good one, so he decided to purchase it.

The storekeeper was adding up the prices of the supplies Nathan had selected when he noticed two other men who entered the store. Nathan hardly paid much attention to them at first, but he thought they appeared grubby. They looked as rough and dirty as any he could remember. But there was something odd about them. He glanced back at the storekeeper, who seemed a bit nervous having them in his store.

Nathan began to worry about his mule outside unattended. Men such as these might just make off with his recent investment while he was engaged in his business inside, unaware and unable to see the goings on out there. He felt suddenly anxious to conclude his shopping and return to his animal, uneasy about leaving it alone for anything beyond a few minutes. And those seedy rogues seemed strangely suspicious the way they didn't inspect products to buy, but instead appeared curiously occupied with his purchases. He forced himself to ignore them, and count his money.

He left the store with almost more than he could carry, hanging the saddle over his left arm and shoulder, with his new rifle, two boxes of ammunition, rope, canteens, tin cup, axe, small shovel, kettle, saw, gold pan, spurs, bridle, bit, saddle blanket, and other smaller gear rolled together, along with the shoulder bag he already had, into three wool blankets, with a canvas tarpaulin on the outside, and everything tied together with a length of rope, and this huge bundle balanced on his right shoulder. He was glad his mule wasn't far from the door.

The mule, though anxious, had not been bothered. Once outside the store, Nathan took to reorganizing his supplies, and saddling the mule to check out how everything was going to fit. He was pleased with the way the load was going to ride, once he had it balanced and adjusted.

He thought he'd heard those two men exit the store behind him, but by the time he had a chance to cast down his burden and look back, he saw no sign of them.

He opened his canvas-wrapped load of provisions and sorted through it, deciding which items to pack back up, and which he might need left out during his travel. The revolver was the first thing to be removed from the pack, and he tucked it under his belt. If any ruffians were to threaten any trouble, the display of the capped and loaded gun might be enough to clear his way without harassment. And if they were brazen enough to pursue him regardless, it would be close at hand where he could call on it, and that was where he decided it should remain from now on.

But he didn't see those characters again all day. Their curiosity must have been satisfied, or perhaps they took note of his ready sidearm. In any case, he was certain by their demeanor they had something on their minds contrary to his own well being, and now it appeared their course had been diverted for whatever reason.

At this point he didn't have much money left. He didn't want to begin his journey without some food provisions, however, and he made a stop at a butcher shop where he purchased ten pounds of beef cut into strips and well seasoned. The man said he could have them smoked and cured by the following morning, and Nathan agreed to have him do it. And not far down the street he purchased some coffee, hardtack, salt, dried peaches, and several tins of beans. By then he was nearly broke, but these staples would sustain him for awhile, without weighting down the mule excessively.

On the second morning following his arrival in California, Nathan, after packing and re-packing his supplies until he felt confident his load was organized, efficient, and carefully balanced over the back of his mule and secured properly, left Sacramento in the coolness of the early hours, and headed east toward the hills, the way he'd plotted on his map.

He knew it'd be a couple of days before he would be well up into those hills, but he had no reason to hurry. The low lands in the valley were sprinkled with an occasional homesteader's farmhouse, and he didn't endeavor to follow any particular road, but traveled line of sight as much as the terrain of the countryside would permit.

His first day's travels did not present any particular difficulties. The weather was hot, but he was able to water the mule at a small creek about midday, and fill his own canteens. And there was plenty of good grazing for the animal where he chose to make camp. He guessed they'd done eight or nine miles, maybe as much as ten, but he didn't want to push too hard, at least not during the warmest part of the day. He expected to be camping on higher ground by the third night out.

He made a small fire and burned the driest dead branches and twigs he could find, then made his bedding of blankets laid atop a mound of grasses he'd collected. The sky looked clear, so he made no effort to put up any sort of shelter.

Not even an hour before the sun went down he noticed a faint column of gray smoke rising some thousand yards to a mile west of him, from roughly the direction he had come. The trees were scattered enough and not especially tall, most of them, so he was able to see the smoke from his location.

Somebody's camp? Could also be trailing from a house chimney, but he didn't remember passing a dwelling in that area. He wondered who would be camped within a mile of his own camp. Cattlemen possibly, but he didn't hear the usual sounds associated with a cattle drive. And it wasn't likely to be Indians. They were rarely that careless these days.

He kept his own fire small, and he was confident that it didn't produce much of a signature. Certainly nothing that could be seen a mile away. Whoever was camped yonder, they took less care and built a larger smoking blaze.

He rolled up into his blankets when darkness came, and stared up into the stars overhead, contemplating the journey laid out before him and the days that would follow. This one had been a full one, and he felt ready for a good rest. The silhouette of his mule, currently motionless next to a small tree to which it was tethered, was the last thing he could remember before dropping off into sleep. And it was a comforting sight, for he knew that if anyone or anything approached, the animal would be alerted before he would, raising such a fuss as to wake him promptly.

The morning arrived in the blink of an eye, owing to the quality of his rest during the night, and he was up getting the small fire going for the morning coffee before the full glow of the sun could be felt. He felt well rested and ready for the day, and after two cups of coffee and several bites of smoked beef, he broke camp and saddled up for an early start.

He had him a reasonable view of the mountains' foothills by this time, and he knew he'd be among them soon. By the time the baking sun was high overhead, he and his mule would be several miles closer. And it was all he could think about now – reaching those mountains he'd dreamt about for such a long time. Those foothills would be a gradual climb that was to begin very soon. He could feel his heart thumping enthusiastically in his chest. He could see the foothills now. Those mountains couldn't be far off.

CHAPTER II

The day had grown hot with the mid-afternoon sun singeing the landscape. By now the foothills appeared close, almost close enough to reach out and touch. Yet there were some miles between Nathan and the high rocks, and he considered making camp soon before the terrain changed drastically.

His eyes began to discern a trail of dust rising among a cluster of cottonwoods possibly five-hundred yards in the direction he was headed; he expected there to be a creek running through that area, where those trees were, and possibly a road paralleled it. He thought about filling his canteens there, as he'd almost completely drained them after hours of travel in mostly open country, unsheltered from the sun. Someone was apparently riding toward him from there, but the growth was tall enough to obscure his view of that area presently.

His first thought was of that camp smoke he'd spotted the prior evening, but this rider (or riders) whoever it was, was approaching from a different direction. That camp had been behind him, but this dust was kicking up ahead of him.

The object of his attention soon revealed itself as a lone rider on a pony, not apparently concerned with or aware of his presence at first, until he realized he was suddenly discovered, and then the rider approached him directly.

Nathan had a very strange feeling about this encounter. There was something going to happen he hadn't counted on, he sensed, and it was going to alter his course somehow, and that was a troubling thought. He couldn't imagine anything that could divert him from his chosen path. It was a weird feeling, and he couldn't understand why he felt it, but as soon as he was able to clearly see the approaching rider, he quickly dismissed it as foolish nonsense. The sun must be getting to him, he thought.

At about a hundred yards distant he perceived his recent visitor was a young lady; she appeared to be younger than he. And even at that distance her feminine attributes were unmistakable – her delicate frame and soft yellow hair that seemed to flow out from under her hat, fluffed by the wind of riding. She was not riding her pony in the more traditional manner of a lady. She sat in the saddle the same way he did, and her dress was that of a man, wearing durable trousers instead of a lady's dress. And over her small shoulders hung a fringed buckskin shirt, with her head topped by a brimmed hat to shade her pretty face.

When she spotted him she rode closer where she could boldly address him, showing no hint of caution that he was a stranger.

"Why do you trespass on my father's land, Mister?" She demanded upon arriving within normal vocal range of him.

His eyes met hers as he drew reins to stop at the question. Then he looked to one side and the other.

"Didn't see any fences nor posted signs." He said. "Wasn't aware this was private land. I merely wander toward those mountains yonder." He nodded to the foothills.

"Please relay to your father my sincerest apology, Miss, and direct me, if you would, in the direction of the nearest border where I may remove myself from his property directly."

She did not respond immediately. Her curious eyes were too busy inspecting his handsomely rustic form, noticing that nearly half of his face carried a two-day's growth of hair, as he hadn't shaved since the morning before when he left Sacramento, and the dark stubbles accentuated his masculine features, which she found strangely appealing.

"What is it that awaits you in those mountains so important," she inquired curiously "that it has you wandering over the land like a lost sheep, loaded down with enough provisions to carry you to the North Pole and back?"

"I seek my fortune in gold up in those hills. It awaits me, and I am compelled to go up there and claim it."

She laughed at his response, presuming he said it with sarcastic humor. Her laughter became rather contagious when he thought about how silly his words sounded even to himself.

After the mutual outburst of emotional humor subsided, he again asked the way to the nearest edge of the property.

Her mind searched for an excuse not to send him off so quickly. "My father would think it most impolite of me to usher off a visitor without inviting him to stay for supper. How far have you come already? You must be starved."

She was enchanted, and anxious to learn more about this young stranger who appeared, as if out of thin air, within the boundaries of the ranch. She recognized this encounter as a rare occurrence so far removed from even the closest neighbors, and she'd never seen a young man who captivated her mind the way Nathan did, though she struggled to conceal her immediate infatuation.

He was no less interested in what he was looking at, and he too tried not to let it show. But it was a challenge for him to avoid staring once he saw her up close, once he had a clear view of the face shaded by her hat. Beautiful was the only word that came to his mind. Beautiful enough to take his breath away, if he wasn't careful.

"I sure could eat something," he said, after a long stretch of silence "though I hate to impose."

"No imposition. Really, Mister…?"

"Clayburn. Nathan Clayburn. Friends usually call me Nate. How should I address you, Miss?"

"Emily. I'm Emily Thibault, and this is the Thibault Ranch. Ours is the largest ranch in this part of the valley. Father owns almost three sections. Let me show you to the house, and you can meet my father."

"I've seen some ranches, Miss, and worked on a few. Can't say I ever saw one like this." He explained, looking about him, noticing how everything he could see wasn't much but raw land left natural in partially wooded rolling hills.

"Looks more like a regular ranch closer to the house." She said. "Come on, I'll show you."

He followed her lead, and when they reached the cottonwoods, he noticed the shallow brook he expected to find there, almost hidden among tall grasses, and there was a road; a private dirt pathway that did some winding through the trees that eventually opened up to where the heart of the ranch lay, and he noticed some open pasture, livestock, horse stables, barn, another building, and finally the large Thibault residence, which was a huge log structure two stories high, surrounded on all four sides, it appeared, by a vast covered porch.

The view from the house was of the immediate meadow and pasture below, beyond which to the east the foothills of the Sierras rose from the earth like mounds imitating giant crawling beasts, crawling up into the hills.

On the porch he saw a husky middle-aged woman beating dust from a rug with the handle of a broom.

"That's Mrs. Rhodes." Emily said, observing that he noticed her, as they rode up toward the hitching rail where they would picket their animals. "She's our housekeeper and maid. She's been with us for ten years, since we lost mother to fever in a hard year. She's raised me like her own daughter, Mrs. Rhodes has. Her first name's Anita, but we all call her Ann."

The woman looked up and saw Emily, and her new company. Nathan tipped his hat to her as he rode alongside Emily to the rail. They dismounted and tethered their animals, and Nathan removed the load from his mule's back and lowered it to the ground to give his creature what he expected would be a short rest.

Nathan was directed by Emily through the massive entrance. Mrs. Rhodes followed them in, anxious to welcome the visitor with her full attention. She was also curious about this stranger.

"Ann," said Emily "this is Mr. Clayburn. He is currently on a voyage to the mountains where he plans to do some prospecting. I met him along the way, and I've invited him to have supper with us."

Nathan removed his hat and took his seat where he was directed, in a room that was something of a large foyer with windows and a good amount of light within, and with the kitchen area at one end, around the great stone fireplace. Nathan marveled at the massive logs that composed the walls of the house. He thought about how many horses would be needed to move such trees to the building site.

"Where is father?" Emily asked her housekeeper. "He should mcet Mr. Clayburn."

"He went to help round up that mustang the Haskins summoned him about earlier. He's over in their field. Started off right after you left."

"Oh, Ann, why didn't he tell me he was going over there today? He knew I wanted to go along, too." Emily's face showed her disappointment in being left out.

"He asked me to fetch you right after the neighbors came by to round him up, but you'd already ventured off with your pony. Was a last-minute thing, I'm sure. Seems you found a mustang of your own." Mrs. Rhodes glanced over at Nathan.

Emily's look of disappointment faded quickly when she turned her attention again to Nathan, and she was no longer concerned about hiding her elation since meeting him on the range. She smiled when his eyes completed their curious scan of the huge room and met hers, and then he began to break a smile of his own, which caught her in a mild trance.

In his casual survey of the room, he noticed the various wall decorations and pieces of furniture that helped compose the general atmosphere. Hanging on an open space of wall was a portrait of a lady with a striking resemblance to Emily. He presumed it was that of her mother. He noticed the tall standing grandfather clock near the stairs leading up to the second floor, which formed something of a balcony, and the old English musket hanging above the fireplace. It was an old flintlock, probably a Brown Bess. Nathan thought it looked majestic above the fireplace like that.

"When do you expect him home?" Emily asked Ann.

"Your father requested that I have supper ready by the four o'clock hour. I don't expect him home before half past three."

"That's more than an hour from now." Emily observed, glancing over at the clock. "Nate," she said, addressing Nathan by his nickname as casually as if she'd known him for years "will you accompany me to the pond down beyond the garden? Something down there I would like to show you. I think you'll find it perfectly entertaining."

Mrs. Rhodes looked at Nathan, waiting anxiously with Emily for his answer. He looked at her, as if soliciting her approval, and she nodded. His eyes then shifted back to Emily.

"Of course I will, Miss Emily, I'd be delighted."

He followed her out the door and down the graveled path bordering a large vegetable garden. They both were thinking the same thing; that their boots and spurs were better suited to riding than hiking down a narrow trail, but neither made a verbal remark regarding it. Each also entertained other thoughts more extensively occupying their blissful minds.

Nathan was thoroughly captivated by his energetic companion, who seemed in her youthful animation almost childlike, but with a confidence suggesting a degree of maturity. And he couldn't help wondering about her age. Was she a mere child of fifteen or sixteen, or could she be as much as eighteen years old? Even at twenty, if that were possible, such a lady would appear hardly older than a girl of sixteen. And if she was no older than sixteen, her demeanor contained more poise and independence than most twenty year-olds he'd met, indeed.

Captivated was he by the way her silky golden hair fluttered in a stirring breeze, reflecting flashes of sunlight that left yellow spots on the pictures in his brain. The pristine skin of her face and hands was not pale like that of other young girls, many of whom spent too much time indoors, but instead lightly browned from occasional exposure to sunlight, a result of her obvious love of the outdoors. He saw her as an enthusiastic, inspiring creature, as magnificent in his eyes as those mountains of his imagination. She had a wild freedom in her spirit that grabbed hold of him and wouldn't let go. He couldn't have ignored it if he'd tried – it was there like the warmth of the afternoon sun.

And the same kind of electricity was within her to an equal degree, for she found him uniquely irresistible in ways she couldn't dream of articulating.

Both kept their impressions to themselves for the moment, still strangers in the scope of time they'd been acquainted. But even as short as their time together had yet been, there remained something strangely eternal about their discovery of one another, and both felt an almost spiritual connection between them. Neither could understand it, because neither had ever felt it before.

"Shhh…" She softly uttered, pressing a finger over her lips, and pointing toward the little pond now visible through a scattering of fruit trees.

Nathan strained to see what she was pointing out, and suddenly took notice of a duck boating itself along on the water, followed by four tiny ducklings; a mother with her young trailing behind her in a perfect line.

"Aren't they beautiful?" She whispered, watching the wild things carrying on with their own business undisturbed. "Occasionally waterfowl vacation here. This family of five has only recently come around. I check on them every day, to make sure no hawks get any of those little ones."

"They sure are." He agreed. "Like so much else I've noticed about this place. Those ducklings should be safe enough with you looking after them. Their lives are worthy of envy."

In a forward move that caught Nathan completely by surprise, Emily grabbed his right hand and assertively towed him directly to a shadier area under a huge oak, where she compelled him to sit down in the cool tall grass next to her. And he interpreted this move, by its bold initiative, as an act granting him license to kiss her on the lips, and he seized the occasion without a breath of hesitation.

The rest of the universe seemed to stand still. She made no effort to conceal her enjoyment of the moment, and the two remained pleasantly adhered to each other for quite awhile, neither feeling at all anxious to interrupt their delightful connection.

After finally relaxing their hold on each other, they both sank to rest themselves on an elbow in the soft earth where they could gaze at each other like two strangers enchanted with their new acquaintance.

Emily giggled, reflecting on what had just occurred. Nathan shared her giddy mood, expressing himself simply with a quiet smile.

"Who are you, Nathan Clayburn?" She wondered aloud. "Where did you come from? What are your parents like?" She tried to imagine what kind of people cultivated such a man as she had in her sights.

"I never knew my parents." His blissful expression changed to a more serious one. "I don't know where they are, or whatever became of them. My grandfather would never tell me that. He always avoided the subject, like some kind of plague. He raised me. He passed on last September, but he was a great man. I should strive to be half the man he was."

"Please tell me about him, then." She interrogated, desiring to learn what human qualities Nathan esteemed.

"My grandfather was a frontiersman who feared nothing in the world. He taught me a lot of great things. His mother and father were Christian folks, and devout in their faith. They named him Gabriel, after The Lord's messenger archangel. Gabriel Clayburn. If I'm ever blessed with a son, I hope to name him Gabriel, after my grandfather. After a great man."

"It's a fine name, Nathan. And he must've been a special kind of man, the way you speak of him. Maybe you're a lot like him. Some things are hereditary, they say."

"I sure hope they're right, then." He said.

"Oh Nate – Nathan Clayburn, you are a mystery. But how can it be that we have just met an hour ago, and already I feel as if…"

"As if we have always known each other?" He finished her question for her. She leaned back into the grass, looking up at the evening sky.

"But how many years would it take for this?" She asked. "Would we feel like this after twenty years? I am certain you could not be more familiar to me after a lifetime. And yet, there is so much I do not know about you.

"I feel as though my life has been frightfully incomplete until this very day, when I encountered you out there hopelessly lost." She continued, staring up at the clouds overhead. "And after all these years…"

"Lost? I would hardly say I was lost." He interrupted again. "And you speak of past years like you've endured a century. Just how old exactly are you, Emily? Seventeen, maybe?"

"Seventeen and a half!" She snapped defensively, emphasizing the word half. "I'll be eighteen in November, for your information. Why? How old are you?" She sat up and looked at him, as if posing herself to prepare for an unpleasant lecture about her age. She seemed especially sensitive about that, which he'd almost half expected, but he was curious nevertheless.

"Twenty-four." He stated calmly, then pausing to contemplate it. "That puts nearly seven years between us!"

"Well, I don't see why a person's age has to be so darned important, anyway." She grumbled, dropping back into the grass to stare up into the sky once again.

"Suppose you're right about that." He said. "Just that society puts stock in it. I figure that's only because society doesn't know too many ladies like yourself."

She quietly reveled in the compliment, but her eyes seemed to show a sense of delight, betraying her hopes of concealing it. She didn't look at Nathan, but kept her focus on those few clouds high above them.

"I was told my Aunt Cynthia was herself married at sixteen." She referred to the only example she knew involving a youthful romance, for setting a suitable precedence.

"And how did her marriage fare?" He asked with an obvious hint of skepticism.

"Now Mr. Clayburn," she replied, suddenly growing a bit annoyed with the whole subject "if our age difference should be of such a monumental dilemma that you see it proper for us to dismiss ourselves of each other's company, please say so now, before I lose command over my own heart, with the most devastating of consequences."

"Indeed, it might already be too late for my heart, Miss Emily. I was engaged to be married less than a month ago, and she was all of twenty-two, and well refined in many ways, but I did not feel anything like this about her."

His admitting to feeling something hung over the awkward silence that followed. It wasn't a surprise. They shared an undeniable attraction to one another, and a strange bond had already begun to form between them. They both felt it, all right. But it was so early. They were still strangers really. This verbal acknowledgement of what they both were feeling rang like a profound revelation, and turned their strangeness into familiarity in an instant. She heard his words as a declaration, and though common sense told her that such words so soon were out of their proper time, she liked what she heard.

But he immediately regretted saying what he said, realizing he'd blurted it out without giving thought to it. He started to remember what his grandfather always told him about thinking before speaking. It was practical advice that could keep a man out of trouble.

An unmeasured duration passed without either of them speaking a word. But the silence was not entirely uncomfortable for either of them, to their surprise. They felt comfortable enough without words.

At last Nathan spoke, breaking the long silence.

"How do just the three of you manage this whole ranch? Or do you have siblings to share the work?"

"No, I'm father's only child. He would have liked having a son to follow in his footsteps, and to help with the ranch, but that wasn't to be."

"Well," Nathan remarked "the three of you do a mighty fine job keeping this place orderly and apparently well maintained, from what I can see."

"Oh," she explained "we've got great help. Stewart Bell works for father. Or, I should say he really works *with* father. The two are almost inseparable at times.

"He's older than my father, but has served him faithfully since before I was born. Stew's a hard working hand, and even as old as he is, he's healthy and strong as an ox. I don't know what we would ever do without him."

"I've known men like that." Nathan said. "As reliable as a Swiss clock, and never stopping until their work day ends. Those are a rare breed."

"Stew's a curious one, though." She added. "Was many times offered a room of his own in my father's house, but he prefers the hay loft in the barn, where he's always resided. He helped raise that barn many years ago, and it's familiar surroundings for him. He takes his supper down there, too, in spite of regular invitations to join the rest of us at the kitchen table. He prefers the company of animals to that of people, he says."

Nathan's hand found a pebble, and he gave it an overhand throw toward the pond, feeling satisfied with a splash somewhere near the middle. The ducks had since paddled their way up the tiny brook that fed the pond, and he made certain they were in the clear before throwing the stone. He turned to Emily as if his attention to her story had not been diverted.

"I can understand that." He said. "Animals make for excellent company usually, with simple concerns and honest dispositions. I think I understand this Stewart fellow."

Just then Mrs. Rhodes' voice was heard summoning them up to the house. Mr. Thibault had returned, she announced, and supper was very nearly ready.

As they made their way back up the hill, Nathan anticipated an awkward greeting from Emily's father, expecting to meet a man understandably suspicious of him; a stranger fraternizing with his daughter, his very young daughter, on his own land.

But he was surprised to encounter the very opposite of what he expected, for Emily's father was a cordial and truly good-natured gentleman who offered him a warm welcome.

"Who's this young man my Emily's invited to share supper with us?" He called out from the front porch, as they approached the house, his hand extending to shake Nathan's, with a welcoming smile.

"Nathan Clayburn, Sir. And your Emily has told me so much about your magnificent ranch. I am simply awe-struck by everything I've seen here."

"Come! Let's go inside and make ourselves comfortable at the table before the mosquitoes make a meal out of us. Ann has the food almost ready." He ushered the two inside and they all took their seats around a stout split-log table, which perfectly matched the rest of the rustic atmosphere within.

"I see you've got yourself a healthy animal out there, Mr. Clayburn. What is that one, sixteen hands maybe?"

"Sixteen plus an inch. A john mule. He's been with me for only two days, but he's been real good. I don't believe I could have found a better animal. Bought him from Carl

Lewiston out of Sacramento, who claims he's a product of a fine Andalusian Jack and a thoroughbred mare, though he doesn't have papers."

"Well I wouldn't doubt it for a minute." Mr. Thibault said. "Must've fetched a strong price, a mule like that. Did you have him shod with a new set of shoes before setting out?"

"Actually, he currently wears no shoes at all. We didn't always shoe our mules back in Missouri, at least those we used to plow the softer fertile fields. If we meant to take them on a hard packed road much, we'd usually put shoes on for that, but… Well, with those dense hooves and all, and I won't have access to a farrier where I'm headed. Just figured it wouldn't be practical."

"Not wanting to tell you what you should do, mind you, but you might consider it. Ann here tells me you're headed up into the Sierras. Lots of rocky terrain that way. We've got the best farrier inside a hundred miles, ol' Stew out there in the barn. He'd be more'n happy to shoe him for you. I'll talk to him about it after supper, if you want me to. Stew's never happy unless he's fussing over putting an animal right."

"I'd be grateful to him." Nathan answered.

Mrs. Rhodes served their supper, aided by Emily after setting the table. Lamb chops and baked potatoes served with home-churned butter made for a genuine feast for Nathan, and he had to consciously restrain himself to avoid the appearance of a glutton. He relished every bite.

"I didn't know you were going out to catch the mustang today, Father." Emily said. "I would liked to have joined in that fun."

"I didn't know myself until Cecil Haskins showed up here this mornin', insisting I ride out to his place. Stew went with me. I tried to round you up, Princess, but you'd already gone out."

"Well, did you catch him?" She could bear the suspense no longer.

"No. Not this time. He's a little faster than we figured. We might try again tomorrow. But it's just as well you didn't go with us today. We ran into a couple real bad characters on our way back – on this ranch.

"I kindly requested they find their way off the ranch. That's when they started getting threatening-like. One reached for his sidearm, but Stew was a bit faster with that Remington of his. No shots were fired, fortunately. But I was mighty glad old Stew was nearby. I'm just not as fast as I used to be. Not sure I'd be here now telling about it if Stew hadn't been there. These were the filthiest, sorriest looking two devils I've seen around here in a long while."

"Sounds like two I ran across in Sacramento." Nathan noted. "Something wicked about them I perceived. But what are the odds they followed me? Why would anyone want to follow a newcomer into the foothills? They don't have any reason to think I know where I'm going, or where to find gold. Haven't found mine just yet."

"Ah." Mr. Thibault dismissed his concern. "May not be following you. May not even be the same two you saw. But it ain't important. Plenty scoundrels in the world. It's a prudent practice to keep your guard up." He took a bite and chewed, swallowing fast to finish his point.

"Those mountains in the distance serve as a hide-out to more than a few hard men and dangerous outlaws. That's important to remember during your travels. I see you pack a hogleg. Hopefully you know how to use it. Might help you out of a tight spot one day. But you don't ever want to let your guard down in those mountains.

"I should insist that Emily keep a shooter close at hand on her wanderings on her pony. Already taught her the proper loading and firing of my Colt Navy revolver."

"I'm a crack shot, Father says." She proudly boasted.

"I certainly would dare not wager against it, considering all that I've been privileged to witness since meeting you, Miss." Remarked Nathan.

Mr. Thibault couldn't help laughing at that. "As you've noticed, she's not a creature to be kept indoors. That's her father's bloodline. Her mother was quite the opposite."

"Would that be Emily's mother's portrait on the wall?" Nathan asked.

Her father nodded "Never met another like her on this crazy earth." He said with a melancholy look in his eyes. "Except little Princess; she's got her mother's spirited personality. And she looks a lot like her mother now that she's growing up. Biggest difference seems to be Emily's attraction to wild things. Never saw that in her mother."

"She was attracted to you, Father." Emily interjected. "Everyone says you were wild in your prime."

He smiled. "Yes, I suppose so." He thought about it further. "Why, there might be more of your mother in you than I ever considered."

"Would you care for a second helping, Mr. Clayburn?" Offered Mrs. Rhodes, noticing that Nathan's appetite was ambitious.

"I think I better put the brakes on before I gorge myself beyond what my mule is willing to carry. But it's been a mighty long time since I've eaten a meal anything like this. You're a fine cook, Mrs. Rhodes, and I'm grateful for the opportunity of finding it out firsthand."

"I do hope you'll allow yourself a night's rest here before resuming your travel." Mr. Thibault persuaded him. "Not a lot of sense in pitching your camp in the dark whilst a house like ours has empty guest rooms."

"How will I ever repay your hospitality?" Nathan asked in genuine awe with the friendly treatment he was receiving.

"Nonsense. It's something of a rare treat for us to have guests these days." Mr. Thibault assured him.

Mrs. Rhodes and Emily began clearing the table of plates, and Nathan stood up to help with the chore of cleaning dishes, as was the usual custom growing up in his grandfather's house, as they never had a maid to help with such chores. His grandmother passed away when he was very young, so the two bachelors were forced to fend for themselves for everything. Nathan was not accustomed to being waited on.

As soon as Nathan was up with his empty plate in his hand, Emily put her hand on his arm, prompting him to sit back down.

"We've got it, Nate. Thanks." She said. "I'd be happy if you would stay and visit with my father awhile. He does so enjoy your company."

Nathan eased back into the chair. Mr. Thibault removed two pipes from a holder and offered one to Nathan. He accepted it, more out of trying to be polite than actually wanting to smoke. He conjured up an image in his head of sharing a peace pipe with an Indian chief. Surely there were similarities here. He had smoked a pipe before, once when he was younger trying to act grown up, but he never acquired much of a taste for tobacco. He decided he would try his best to enjoy it on this eve, making the most of an enjoyable visit.

While Emily and Mrs. Rhodes carried the dirty dishes in baskets outside where they could scrub them with well water, Nathan followed Mr. Thibault down to the barn to be introduced to Stewart, who happened to be brushing his own riding mare.

"Stew," said Mr. Thibault "this here is Nathan Clayburn. He'll be taking his mule up into the hills, and the animal needs shoes. Thought you might take care of that for him, if you would."

"Sure thing, Jake. I'll put them hooves right. Just about done brushin' down Rosie here. How do you do, Mr. Clayburn? If you'd kindly walk your mule 'round, I'll get my tools ready. Nothin' I like better'n this whole world than shoein'. Mighty satisfyin' knowin' a critter's fixed up proper. Jake most likely done told ya I'm a natural-born hoof doctor."

"In fact he did say something to that effect." Remarked Nathan. "But I'll have to remain in your debt until I come into some means, since getting outfitted temporarily drained my reserves."

"No, Sir. I couldn't even consider makin' a charge to a guest at the Thibault Ranch. Don't you fret over it. I been a shoein' since I's five years old, and like I said, ain't nothin' I enjoy more."

Nathan collected his mule and led him down to the barn, leaving him in Stewart's care. Then he joined Mr. Thibault on the porch, where they resumed their smoking, sitting on the steps where they could watch the sun go down. The tobacco smoke seemed to discourage hungry mosquitoes from bothering them much.

Emily was inside the house talking with Mrs. Rhodes, about exactly what he couldn't decipher from where he sat.

"Mr. Clayburn, er, Nathan," Emily's father began, staring off toward the distant hills "it's a long road you've got ahead of you. You might find your gold out there somewhere. Some have found gold in those hills, and in those streams where the snow runoff carves channels into the earth. Still some have worked awful hard at it and never found any at all."

He took a draw on his pipe and puffed two little clouds of smoke that hung in the air. Nathan remained silent, listening and thinking about what the man said. He took a draw himself and puffed once.

"The thing is," continued Mr. Thibault "a man's got to plant him some roots somewhere. A plant without roots gets blown away by a strong wind, and leaves nothing behind. Its value is less than a plant with roots that can grow tall and live long. The same is true with a man. If he neglects putting down his roots somewhere, he'll find himself wanderin' the planet until his days end, and he won't have a thing to show for his life. It's hard to see it that way when you're young, I know, but you sure do see it when you get on in years."

Still Nathan sat quietly listening, trying to determine exactly what it was Mr. Thibault was trying to tell him.

"Point I'm tryin' to make, Son, is that this here's a mighty big ranch for just the four of us to manage now, and I'm not getting' younger. We could sure use an extra hand around here, if you'd be wanting a job. I've noticed how Emily's taking a liking to you, and we've got plenty of room." He took another draw on his pipe. "But it's just somethin' you might think on."

"It's a grand offer indeed, Mr. Thibault. If I didn't already have my sights trained on those mountains, I'd take you up on it. I surely would. But I've been a long time planning."

"I understand. And I admire your determination. But if you don't find what you're looking for out there, my offer still stands."

The ringing of Stew's hammer shaping horseshoes on the anvil sounded from the barn, and crickets' chirping grew louder with the approaching nightfall, reminding Nathan of an orchestra.

The owner of the ranch noticed his young guest's eyelids looked heavy from a long day of traveling.

"Won't keep you up all night, as I know you've had you a long trek already and you'll likely be wantin' to set out early tomorrow. But I'd have you think about what I told ya. Those mountains are inviting, but they're hard, and they're wild. Lots of things can happen to a man in the wilderness. Life on this ranch has its share of work, won't tell you different, but it's a good life here."

Mr. Thibault then fetched Ann to show Nathan a guestroom and where he could wash up. Nathan moved his pack into the tack room for shelter in case of an unexpected thunder shower during the night, and then followed Mrs. Rhodes to his quarters to retire for the night.

After washing the sweat and range dust off himself, Nathan relaxed on the bunk in the guestroom he'd been shown, and he put the shutters at the window open to allow the fresh evening breeze in. This was heaven, he thought. Never had he dreamed of such friendly hospitality in this part of the country. These Thibaults were a special kind of people. That was surely clear to him.

He had very nearly dropped off to sleep when he heard the door latch slowly lifting. He instinctively reached for his revolver, which he'd set on the little stand next to the bed, but as soon as he did he thought about how ridiculous it seemed to be reaching for a gun while he was a guest in someone else's home. He remained motionless and silent, waiting to learn whom it would be so quietly entering. Perhaps it was the housekeeper, he considered, bringing him extra blankets in case it might cool down later, while hoping not to disturb his rest.

As the door gradually swung inward, it creaked on its hinges, and soon he saw silhouetted in the moonlight beaming through the open window the form he recognized. It was not the housekeeper, but Emily, and she was trying to walk softly and quietly, closing the door behind her.

"Nate, are you asleep yet?" She whispered.

"I'm awake." He answered almost as quietly. "What brings you to this room?"

"I can't sleep. Are you really leaving tomorrow?" She asked.

"Yes. I should be gone before the sun glows on the eastern horizon. Hope to get some distance before the hottest part of the day."

"Oh Nate," she cried "I cannot stand to spend this night without you! I know I must be insane, and we've been acquainted such a short time, but I... I cannot sleep. Not while you're still here, in the same house. If I cannot spend these last hours in your arms, I *will* go insane."

In the dim light he saw her silky nightshirt slide off her frame into a pile on the pine floor next to her bare feet; her naked body appeared bluish-gray in the light of the moon, and her blond hair seemed to flow like water in a waterfall, gently over her smooth form. He thought she looked quite a lot like an angel glowing out of a shadow, the way the moonbeam reflected light off her skin. In an instant he was certain that this was the most beautiful picture he had ever seen. A wave of mixed feelings suddenly assaulted his senses.

"Emily! I am a guest in your father's house, and he has shown me extraordinary hospitality. What kind of man would I be to betray his goodwill?"

"I love my father more than my own life." She affirmed. "I would rather die than hurt him. But this is not about him at all. If he were to know my own heart at this moment... It would be the most cruel thing to deny me. My father might not understand. He might not know my heart, but he is not a cruel man. I cannot deny my own heart."

She climbed into the bed and nestled close, arresting his inclination to resist her affection.

"Our time together will be short." He reminded her. "No matter how much I'd like it to last, I am on a path set by destiny, and I won't be diverted by anything short of dying."

"But you will come back, won't you? Once you've found your wealth in gold, or whatever you're looking for, you will return to me?"

"I promise." He assured her. "Hard to imagine how anyone could not. To never return would be the equivalent of retiring to a cold dark chamber eternally void of all joy and happiness. Of course I'll return. I should be away no longer than a month, or possibly two at the very most. Can you bear my absence for that short period?"

"Not with even an ounce of pleasure." She stated, resigning to the unpleasant reality. "But I shall endure every day that you are gone only with the knowledge that you will return, and I will count the lonely days, praying each one that you will decide to return in one month, rather than two."

It was a late hour when Emily quietly tiptoed back to her own room, finally feeling the weight of drowsiness herself. Nathan had already fallen asleep by then, and she left him in his peaceful state, careful to avoid disturbing his seemingly perfect rest.

She felt different now. She had transformed from being a girl into a woman, and she sensed that her life was never going to be the same. She had so much to think about now, but she was too sleepy to think at the moment. What it all meant would have to be figured out the next day, when she could think more clearly.

When she awoke the sun was already up, and the sounds of chopping firewood and voices conversing echoed into her bedroom window, which she'd left open all night for fresh air. She knew the activity was coming from the yard near the barn, and she dressed herself as quickly as she could and ran down the stairs, meeting Mrs. Rhodes before exiting the door.

"Emily, child, what is your rush?"

"Good morning, Ann. What time is it?" She was still wiping the sleep from her eyes, trying to focus on the clock at the bottom of the stairs.

"Half past Seven." Answered the housekeeper. "And this isn't like you to sleep in so late."

"I know. Has Nathan left yet?" There was an anxious tone of dread of the expected answer to that.

"He has. Close to two hours ago. I fried three eggs for him before he went out. But he asked me not to wake you."

Emily ran outside toward the barn, as if hoping by some miracle he'd been held up and she could see him off. But he wasn't still around. Stew and her father were so engaged in their private log splitting competition they didn't immediately notice her presence.

"Nathan's gone already?" She cried in disbelief, desperately hoping to be proved wrong about what she knew.

Jacob Thibault leaned the handle of his splitter maul against the stump he'd been splitting logs on and turned around to face his daughter, speechless for a moment in the knowledge of her heavy disappointment. He said not a word, but she knew the answer, and she threw her arms around him and buried her teary-eyed face in his sweaty shirt. Stew tried to ignore all of it and continue splitting, as always avoiding sticking his nose into the private matters of others. He also saw an opportunity to get ahead on his log count.

"Now you oughtn't to be troubling yourself about it. He's got places he needs to see, and he's come a long way to see 'em." Her father tried his best to console her, knowing full well it wouldn't change her feelings at the moment. "He'll be coming back, you can count on that."

"But how can I be sure of it?" She pleaded.

"Because he's got an eye for you, and nature won't let him take his mind off you very long. It was the same way with me, when I met your mother. So I know he'll be back. I count myself as a pretty good judge of character, and I think I know him pretty well. He's a lot like I was at his age."

Mr. Thibault reached into his pocket and took out a gold plated gentleman's pocket watch and chain. He handed it to Emily.

"You better take this before it gets damaged in my pocket. Almost forget I had it." He told her. "Said it was his grandfather's, and he asked me to give it to you. See? That should tell you something. A man doesn't give his grandfather's watch away to someone he doesn't think mighty highly of."

She took the watch from her father and held it in her hands, treating it like it was a sacred gift from heaven. When she turned it over, she read the name Gabriel Clayburn engraved in script letters on the back. She stood there staring at it for at least a minute, unable to speak, until her father interrupted her trance.

"Now Princess, your pony's been wondering where you've been all morning, and Stew and I have a heap of work to do."

Emily wandered slowly back up to the house, holding the watch in her hand like it was the most important thing in the whole world. The splitting of logs behind her faded into a blur of distant activity, until she no longer heard a sound. Her thoughts were far, far away.

CHAPTER III

"Chances are you won't have much trouble with the Maidu Indians, depending on where you camp, as long as they don't perceive you to be a threat to the security of their village." Mr. Thibault had explained while Nathan saddled up his mule before leaving.

"Bears are common, though, and some of them could give you trouble if you let 'em. If they get a notion there's food to be had in your camp, they can be a real menace. And if you stumble across a mother with her cubs, that can be a problem."

Nathan was in the mountains now. He had located a trail and had followed it up, winding his way higher and higher, with the things Mr. Thibault said nearly nine hours earlier now going through his head. He would want to make camp pretty soon, and he studied the terrain with that in mind.

The trail dropped down to a little brook and then paralleled it for most of a mile. When he reached an area lush with tall grass and shade trees, somewhat level, he decided it would be a good place to stop.

After letting his mule drink and filling his canteens, Nathan tied a rope between two trees and picketed his mule on it, where the animal could graze in the shade. Less than fifty feet away he rigged up a lean-to shelter using the chunk of canvas he'd bought. He strung it up so that its open end faced his mule, where he could keep an eye on him.

This was more of a draw than a valley, but it was grooved down the middle with this mountain stream that was running cold and clear near the campsite. Its running water was louder than the wind through the tops of the trees.

It was cool and shady around the camp, but the sun shone bright on the more open hillsides climbing up out of the draw. The hill appeared steeper on the camp side of the creek, with an unusual rocky outcropping about a hundred and fifty to two-hundred feet higher. The trail appeared to follow around to the top of that. The granite seemed to jet out of the side of the hill, over a lot of thick brush and scattered trees. It looked like a decent position for viewing the area, up on that high ledge. He might explore it after he rested awhile, he told himself.

He was also anxious to try his luck with his gold pan in that little stream. There were still a few hours of daylight remaining, and he would learn all he could of his new environment before nightfall.

He decided that before he did much of anything else, he ought to test his rifle. He only had forty rounds of ammunition for it, but he'd have to expend some of those precious cartridges before he'd have any confidence in the weapon, and the sooner he did that, the better. Ten times that much ammunition would be worthless if the rifle didn't work right, and there was only one way to know. And he would need to know where the rifle's bullets hit in relation to where it was aimed.

Looking around, he found a large standing dead pine with long sections of outer bark missing, exposing smooth sun-bleached wood on areas of its trunk, and it had a dark knotty patch roughly three inches across almost in the center. That would serve as his point of aim, and any hits high, low, or to either side should show up clearly on the light woody surface.

With his axe he harvested two sturdy poles of about three feet in length, the diameter of broom handles, and he lashed them together with a bootlace at about three-quarters their length from one end. By spreading the longer unsecured ends apart like the legs of a bipod and jamming those into the dirt, a rest for the rifle was established.

He'd paced off fifty yards from the tree, and that was where he positioned the rest. Behind that he threw down a rolled up blanket for something to sit on. A box of cartridges was opened and placed where he could access them without moving much.

He folded his handkerchief and stuffed it into the V-notch of the shooting sticks, over which he rested the for-end of the rifle, making final adjustments to the height of the stand until it suited him. This was a comfortable arrangement, and he was able to steady the rifle quite well.

With his right hand he lowered the gun's lever and inserted a .46-caliber cartridge into the chamber, then raised the lever to close the breech, and thumbed back the hammer before aligning the sights. With the stock butted to his shoulder, he settled down to take his first shot.

The roar of the gun stirred the quiet woods, and a thin cloud of burned gunpowder lingered in the afternoon air.

Nathan could hear a crow cawing several hundred yards distant, as if scolding him for disturbing the silence.

The bullet hole appeared on the tree about two inches above the knot. That was an indication his windage was good, if it wasn't just luck, but he might want to make adjustments for elevation.

A proper determination can't be made by only one shot, so he lowered the lever and ejected the empty casing by sliding the button protruding under the for-end to the rear, and then inserted a second fresh cartridge.

He held the same sight picture and applied steady pressure on the trigger. The Ballard belched a second time, and when the air was clear he saw a chunk missing out of the tree in the spot where that first hole had been. Two out of two was better than luck, he decided, and he gathered up his rifle and gear and returned to camp.

Two inches high at fifty yards should put him dead on a little farther out, and he was pleased with how it shot. It also seemed to deliver a good wallop at that distance, and he was confident the rifle would serve him well. The printed advertising on the ammunition boxes boasted three-hundred grain bullets over forty-five grains of high-grade gunpowder. The salesman was probably right about this load being stronger than what those fancy Winchesters and Henry rifles were using. Nathan liked his Ballard just fine.

His mule hadn't seemed to be much bothered by the gun shots, and that was fortunate. If he ever had to take a shot while riding, he wouldn't want the animal to lose his senses to fright. A man never knows when or where he'll have to take a shot, so it's an important concern.

The gun shots had echoed some against the facing hillside; their noise only partially absorbed by the trees. That was something to think about. If any Indians were in the area, they'd likely have heard those shots, alerting them to his presence. That possibility was really impossible to assess, but it warranted consideration, though he could do nothing about it now that he'd already fired the shots. He guessed that if there were Indians about, they'd likely already have known where he was, anyway. The aborigine is known to have that kind of keen awareness in his own environment. Nathan realized that he would have to learn the same ability, if he was going to survive out here.

From experience he knew the importance of keeping his guns clean, and he wasted little time pulling a couple wet rags through the bore of the rifle to wipe away the powder residue and then drying the gun's chamber and barrel with a clean dry cloth.

While it was on his mind, he checked the loads in his revolver. That was important to do periodically, to make sure no caps had fallen loose, and the grease wasn't disturbed over the chambers. Conventional wisdom respecting caplocks recommended keeping fresh loads in their chambers, and keeping them perfectly dry and clean. Everything looked good with the Joslyn, and he tucked it back under his belt.

The afternoon was getting on, and he still wanted to check out that stream. He took up his gold pan and wandered down to the water. He had never actually panned gold before, but back home he had done a bit of practicing using an old ridged pie tin for a pan, and panned tiny bird shot from a bucket of dirt and rocks. He had read about doing that, and he tried it until he had developed a workable technique.

Looking up and down the stream, he contemplated where he would begin. It was somewhat noisy close to the water. Even a small creek like that carries a substantial amount of snow run-off down out of the mountains, and it makes some noise in the process —the perpetual splashing over rocks – water seeking lower ground.

Once a man trains his ear, he can detect things beyond the sounds of the stream. He can teach himself to listen to two things at the same time. Spending time alone in the wild teaches a man many such things. The slow learners often experience an early departure from the natural world. Nathan was determined to hone his woodsman's senses as swiftly as needed, keeping the potential hazards always in the back of his mind, and staying alert just as Emily's father had urged that he constantly do. And that was something else to think about now. Emily was someone to return to, and he was determined that he would, immediately after finding his riches in gold.

James Ballou

He looked for natural gold traps of the kind he'd read about, and took some earth from a matting of exposed roots where the bank was cut by the current, and where tiny pebbles lay trapped along with other soil and debris that had been extracted and moved by the traveling water, finally coming to rest where fate would have him discover it. He tossed a handful of that into his pan and sloshed it around with water, separating the lighter material from the heavier material.

He hadn't been able to afford a rocker or any sluice box. If he started finding good color, he would either attempt to assemble some sort of contraption to serve that purpose, using natural materials and his creativity, or failing that he would ride to the nearest town with as much as he could recover by panning in a reasonable time, and use that to purchase a more efficient contraption. But for the time being, he would be limited to the panning recovery method.

Thoughts of that old timer were going through his head. He wondered where he lived, and how he survived in these mountains. The winters must be brutal, considering how remote this was. If he had a cabin, he'd most likely have to spend all summer just cutting and storing firewood. He'd probably have to smoke an awful lot of meat to sustain him through a whole winter. And if he had to acquire supplies, how would he carry them? If he's got a horse or a mule, how does he keep it fed and watered in this terrain. Might not be such a trick during the greenest part of the year, like right now, but in the winter?

He continued working, panning a handful of dirt from one spot, a handful of creek gravel from another, and so on, sampling different areas of the stream as the afternoon faded into evening, and the sun dipped low behind those trees. He'd worked a good bit of material, but he found no color. He found nothing that resembled yellow gold.

It was much too early to feel any disappointment. He had no reasonable expectations of finding his treasure in this stream. He might have to sample a dozen others before he hit it rich. Even so, he wasn't ready to give up on it just yet. There still *could* be something there, and he hadn't searched it all. The next day would give him more hours of usable daylight, and he would search this stream hard before moving on to another.

Before darkness hindered all visibility, Nathan prepared his camp. He cleared the rocks out of an area on the ground the length and width of his body, and filled in the hole with pine boughs he had harvested with his jackknife. He threw two blankets down over the spot, and that was his bed.

Not more than five feet from his canvas shelter opening was where he lined rocks around a shallow pit he had dug for his fire. He spent the next half hour gathering dry sticks to burn, piling them into a stack within arm's reach.

His fire kit included a carbon steel U-shaped bar, a jagged piece of flint rock, and a small tin full of charred cloth patches. He struck sparks onto a piece of char and blew on it until one of the sparks transformed into a smoldering ember, and this he transferred to a handful of fuzzy tinder he'd prepared by rubbing dry juniper bark between the palms of his hands.

Within seconds he had a small crackling fire climbing the little stack of twigs he'd built, and the satisfying aroma of wood smoke filled his nostrils.

The woods were beginning to cool down noticeably, and he felt the difference the elevation made in the climate. He stuffed his flint and steel kit together with his jackknife into a small linen sack, and tucked this under a heavy rock that he noticed had a depression under it in the ground large enough to store a few things. He found that little hole when he moved the rock to use around his fire pit, but when he saw it he realized it would make a good hiding place for certain small items.

He added a few sticks of wood to feed the fire as it grew, and rolled himself up into his thickest blanket. This had been a longer day for him than the one before it, and he was happy to let it wind down. In the flickering light of the campfire he saw his rifle leaning against one of the trees to which his shelter was strung, and a few yards beyond that his mule stood against a backdrop of mixed conifers. The animal looked asleep, or getting there, as quiet and still as he was.

The evening was tranquil. He knew there'd be a lot of nocturnal activity later in the night, with rodents on the ground and bigger creatures hunting them. A man never sees most of what goes on in the woods at night, but if he did, he'd probably find more activity then than he ever would during the day. Sometimes the evidence of night visitors in a camp were visible in the mornings, like the hoof prints of curious deer left behind in the soft dirt. Nathan wasn't bothered by that. A horse or mule around limits the visits by most intruders, serving as a good alarm system usually for such things as bears or sneaky Indians, which could pose a threat.

Indians. The thought of hostile natives lurking about in the night made it difficult to fall right off to sleep, even as unlikely as he knew that would be. The Maidu, according to Mr. Thibault, weren't as treacherous as Apaches or Comanches, at least they didn't have the same kind of reputation. And even if this was their environment, they'd just as likely be sleeping at night as would any other people, he told himself. The cumbersome revolver pressing against his side nevertheless provided him a little peace of mind, for if anything happened during the night, that forty-four was loaded and ready.

Soon the surrounding trees were shady dark, and the only light was what radiated from his campfire. The gurgling sounds of stream water rolling over stones were the only sounds he could hear, besides the crackling of campfire flames. Sometimes those sounds could play tricks with the imagination, making a man think he hears things deeper into the woods that don't really exist, or possibly obscuring other noises that he should probably pay attention to. The first couple of nights in the wild are usually the hardest for sleeping, until a man becomes more accustomed to his surroundings. Nathan had done his share of outdoor camping before, but these mountains were still rather new to him. This region was a wild and remote place, there was no denying that. It seemed to be everything he could ever hope for.

He didn't stay awake long. He couldn't keep his drowsy eyes open more than a few minutes, and those gurgling sounds from the brook soon faded as he drifted off into a comfortable slumber, his mind too exhausted even to dream.

He knew he hadn't slept long when something woke him. Exactly what it was he wasn't sure. It may have been a noise in the woods. It may have been his own restlessness, but he didn't think so, because those ears on his mule were perked and his dark shape stood with a certain tenseness, barely noticeable in the fading glow of the dying campfire, but noticeable. The beast was aware of something out there in the darkness, and was straining his ears to detect every audible clue. Nathan currently could hear nothing, but something had disturbed his rest, and that same something surely had his mule's attention.

Nathan's eyes strained to scan the perimeter of his camp, but nothing unusual was discernible, and his eyes were tired enough that it was difficult to focus on the shadowy images. And he listened carefully to the sounds of the night, but

47

heard nothing to suggest the stirring of creatures, even the two-legged kind.

Slowly and quietly his right hand reached for the Joslyn until his fingers found the handle, and he gripped the gun as he would to fire it, rolling his thumb over the hammer where he could cock it back swiftly if needed. But after a few minutes of waiting and listening, he didn't hear or see anything new, and his mule seemed to relax. Whatever it was, it must have vanished. It was probably just a deer; a curious critter wandering close enough to get his mule's attention, maybe kicking a branch with a hoof and making just enough noise to startle him out of his sleep.

He felt a little foolish for letting something as harmless as a deer disturb his peace. He was a click of a beat away from having his pistol out and ready for action, and he halfway expected some at first. But now all was quiet other than the trickling water in the nearby stream and the irregular hissing of coals in the fire pit. As sleepy as he felt, he knew he'd have no trouble falling back to sleep.

Morning came sooner than he expected. He realized he must have slept well because he didn't remember waking up again during the night even one time after that early disturbance. He had closed his eyes and then opened them when the early morning had already arrived.

There was just enough light to see everything around camp, but the sun had not yet penetrated the higher branches of the surrounding trees. The air was chilly. Nathan could see his breath, and the glistening wet of morning dew on blades of grass.

He climbed out from his blankets and immediately began stacking twigs for a small fire over which he could heat up water for the morning coffee. And he was hungry. He had bedded down with an empty stomach, being too sleepy to care when evening came, and now had an appetite with a rage. He fumbled through his bags for a strip of jerked beef, and chewed a mouthful while waiting for his pail of water to heat up.

Once he had flames, he tucked the little bag containing the fire kit and knife back under the rock for safe keeping, and warmed his hands over the fire. It crackled and climbed the sticks up to his boiling pot, which hung suspended from a forked branch he had cut the previous afternoon while setting up camp. Soon a hot cup full of black coffee was helping to take the chill out of Nathan's morning, and awaken him to the day ahead.

There was a lot to think on. This creek might have gold in it, even though he hadn't seen color the day before, but he didn't think that was too likely. Even so, the creek was there to be searched, and gold is wherever gold is. It could be anywhere. A mountain stream has as good a chance of trapping gold as anything else, because it's really a natural sluice box, continually passing material over its bedrocks, and eroding the earth over a long path with a chance of cutting into a vein somewhere along the line, if any were there. If any gold remained in these mountains, a stream somewhere should contain traces of it. It would be a mistake not to try every last one he came across.

He would get back to his prospecting soon enough, but he had other matters to focus on first. His curiosity urged him to scout around the area, and learn something about this place. Since he was a youngster he always wanted to explore new places, and he never outgrew the desire. These mountains intrigued him, and he wanted to learn as much as he could about them.

And there would be a lot for him to discover here. There would be trees and plants not common back in Missouri, and there would be wildlife natural to this region alone. He sensed a cornucopia of new discoveries awaited him, and he was eager to find them. Such wonders he'd read about, and they excited him no less than the prospect of finding gold.

With his revolver tucked under his belt, he spent the next half hour or so scouting about the area, finding things unfamiliar to him, and scenes he could never have imagined or envisioned from anything he'd ever read.

He tried to keep mostly within eyesight of his mule in camp, there picketed on that rope he'd strung between those trees. If he tended to stray a bit far, the animal would begin to fuss. He didn't like being left by himself, and that was probably a good thing, Nathan thought, at least out here.

He was also looking for any signs or claim markings. He didn't want to find himself on someone else's claim if he made any discoveries. That could be awfully discouraging. This stream, at least this part of it, looked to be free of any prospector's claim. He could work as much material here as he cared to without such worries. And it didn't look like anyone had been here for a long time. That trail was probably a deer trail, rather than a horse trail.

After returning to camp, he walked his mule down to the water for a drink. The animal drank a long time. Nathan picked out a good spot close by with plenty of green grass for grazing and well shaded by trees where he decided to tether the mule for the morning while he worked his pan in the stream.

By now the sun was an hour up, and the woods were well illuminated. He thought about how picturesque the scenery was here. This seemed something like a dream really, and he had surely spent a long time dreaming about being here long before he left Missouri, and now that he was here, it was almost overwhelming.

He began to feel the first gentle morning breeze sweeping through the branches, spreading the smell of conifers and other vegetation. Birds were beginning to chatter high in those trees. Looking up through an opening to the clear sky over him, he saw a hawk gracefully gliding on an air stream, like a kite high in the sky. It was probably hunting its breakfast.

Nathan knew this was where he wanted to be. Perhaps his lust for gold brought him here, but there was something else. There was a natural beauty in these mountains that just didn't exist in the low lands. And there was that wildness here – a sense of freedom one didn't find on any farm.

There must have been something embedded in his fate that brought him to these mountains. Something unstoppable. He had been driven to this very location, as if he had been meant to come here from the moment he was born into this world. That was how it felt right now, and the feeling was strong.

He collected his pan and returned to the cold running water of the stream where he began processing clumps of material, sloshing away the mud in the current, using a circular motion to separate the light dirt from the heavier gravel. Pan full after pan full he worked material from the creek bottom, as well as from the surrounding dry ground.

This was a different kind of work than anything he'd been used to doing. Unlike baling hay or roping cattle, this activity didn't allow much freedom of movement. It involved wading into the frigid water and staying hunched over a gold pan, straining the eyes to find the tiniest flakes of yellow, pan full after pan full, sometimes long without any encouraging sign of real gold, while one leg or the other usually falls asleep for lack of proper blood circulation. And the hands eventually turn purple working in the numbing cold mountain stream.

This kind of work was going to take some time to get used to, he discovered, and after a little more than an hour of panning without any luck, he decided it was time to take a break and pursue another activity for awhile.

He might try his luck fishing in the little creek. He'd seen a few medium-sized fish zipping out from under a log

51

James Ballou

down across a quiet pool. Trout roasted over the campfire would be a real treat compared to the hardtack and dried beef he'd been eating.

He had no fish tackle with him. It was one of those kinds of things he should have thought to purchase in Sacramento. Even a few hooks would be really useful right now, and hooks never did cost much. But he had so many other things to think about in town, he clean forgot about fish tackle.

It occurred to him that he could fashion a hook out of wood. He'd done that as a young boy along the river when he had no money even to buy fishhooks. Wooden hooks aren't as easy to use, but under the right conditions have been known to work. He had made them work, all right. The kind he and his river pals used to make were simple; they used to call them buttonhooks. They were simply small tough sticks sharpened at both ends and secured by the line in the center. When the fish swallows it with the bait, it tends to wedge its sharp ends into the sides of the fish's mouth, thereby hooking it. They used to make fish stringers the same way, to hold their catch. The little pointed sticks would be passed through the gills like a button through a buttonhole, hence the term "buttonhook". They always worked well.

Such hooks aren't difficult to make using a pocketknife, and Nathan had a good supply of strong waxed linen thread in his sewing kit, which would make a functional fish line.

While he set about hunting up some hard twigs the size and strength he wanted for shaping into hooks, he started reflecting back to the events of the previous several days. His mind became more occupied with a daydream than on his task at hand. He couldn't stop thinking about Emily.

She hadn't been part of his plans. When he set out on his prospector's voyage, he was determined to avoid any such distractions. He had walked away from a relationship, and put that part of his life behind him. All he'd cared about was reaching these mountains and searching them for what he might find. He had no thoughts of meeting someone like Emily. He couldn't have envisioned anything or anyone that could seem nearly as important to him as the Sierra Nevada. But now that he'd met Emily, and become intimate with her, he was beginning to have a struggle focusing on anything else.

And it was strange the way they met. How could he ever have expected anything like that? It was such a strong feeling he had when he met her. It was like he was meant to meet her, like their separate paths were set on a course to merge, somehow by destiny, maybe even before either of them were born. How else could he make any sense of it? They'd shared each other's company for a period of less than twenty-four hours, and yet it seemed as though they'd known one another all their lives. He never knew that kind of feeling before.

He wouldn't be able to stay away for long. She was someone to come back to. And he was beginning to realize that he really wasn't his own free spirit anymore. A fixed destiny seemed to guide him now, more compelling than his urge to wander the hills in search of riches. Or could it be simply that his definition of riches was changing?

His pensive trance was interrupted by the sudden restlessness of his mule. The animal couldn't keep still, and his ears were active – more active even than the night before, and Nathan knew something off in the trees was disturbing him. Maybe there was a bear not far away, or Indians sneaking about, waiting to pounce on him and take his scalp. These weren't supposed to be scalping Indians in these mountains, according to what Jacob Thibault had said, but they could be hostile. Nothing in this part of the country would surprise Nathan. He'd seen enough things already that he never would have expected to see. He knew that out here, anything could be possible.

CHAPTER IV

His right hand instinctively reached for the butt of the Joslyn revolver as he turned around to see what it was that had his mule all worked up. And he heard movement behind him, so he spun around fast, but he was already too late.

"Wudn't 'tempt ta use that thar shooter, if'n I's you, Mister, seein's hows we got us a couple rafles aimed on yer head." The closest one of two men said, while both of them kept big front-loader long guns trained on him.

They seemed to appear out of nowhere. He hadn't heard so much as a leaf crunch under a boot, and he wondered how long they'd been there. Looking at first one and then the other, he immediately recognized them as those two mangy sorts he saw in the general store in Sacramento.

"What do you two want? Haven't found any gold, if that's what you're after."

The farthest one chuckled "Hear that, Leroy? Wishes to divvy his gold up with us, but ain't found none. Now ain't this a kindly feller we run into?"

"Didn't say I'd be wanting to divvy anything up with anyone." Nathan corrected. "Just said I haven't found any gold. But if I had, guarantee sure wouldn't share it with two rogues whose usual manners consist of greeting a lone traveler with the muzzle-end of their rifle barrels. But you don't need those rifles on my account. I'm about my own business. Not looking for trouble."

Clearly insulted by being called a rogue, the man lost his smirk to a more sinister expression. "Now you listen here, we got the drop on ya, and you ain't in no p'sition to be a runnin' yer mouth off.

"Leroy," he turned to the other one "I'll keep a bead on 'im so's you kin bind up those hands an' feet. Git them spurs. Git them boots off, too. Boots is worth somethin'."

The closest one, called Leroy, set his own gun down in the grass and directly approached and yanked the Joslyn swiftly from Nathan's hand, then with its butt raked him across the mouth a hard lick. Nathan stumbled backwards a step, then regained his balance. He hadn't been ready for this. His right hand instinctively covered his mouth, as if to hold the blood from running out, before the man grabbed both his wrists and jerked them together behind his back, binding them tightly with a length of hemp rope.

He immediately understood the degree of misfortune he now encountered, but what could he do about it? These were professional thieves with a lot of practice preying on others. They had no interest in any kind of honest way. They were hard, vicious men. He'd seen their kind before, and they were parasites. They had succeeded in catching him by surprise, and now they would rob him of his hard-earned possessions, then dispose of him so as to hide the evidence of their wicked crime, and prevent him from tracking them down. That was how such ruthless outlaws as these got along in the world. Nathan could smell their foul presence, all right.

He considered plotting a move, but that other rifle was pointed right at his head, and that scruffy character with his finger on the trigger wouldn't be troubled at all by pulling it. That much was obvious. Nathan looked them over carefully, and he was certain that if no guns were involved, he'd be able to whip the breeches off of them both at the same time. They were hard and mean, but they didn't appear exactly agile or physically strong. Years of hard drinking probably took its toll on them, but right now they had the guns, and Nathan didn't.

"You two followed my trail up here from town, didn't you? I remember seeing the both of you back there in the store." Nathan's mouth was bloody, and his lower lip was numb, making his speech awkward. He spit on the ground.

"Watched ya buy supplies lack they was a goin' outa style." Said the man holding the gun, grinning and showing a mouth missing some front teeth. "We says, now here's a feller ta keep a close eye on." He chuckled. "Now them supplies belongs t' us. Yer jest a greenhorn sucker an' a damned fool. Shoulda made yerself more awares, gonna wander 'round this country."

With his wrists bound behind his back and no access to any weapon, Nathan felt almost completely helpless. His only chance of doing anything now would be to use his feet, and kick the closest one as hard as he could, and maybe, just maybe…

It wasn't going to be a workable plan. The other one was too far away to kick, and he still had that rifle aimed on him. Any kind of struggle now would surely earn him a well-placed bullet.

But he knew that his chances of getting out of this mess were slim anyway. These men would most likely cut his throat or hang him before it was all over. And men like these would enjoy the killing. Nathan thought about that. He was a dead man either way, but if he kicked real hard, then at least he could…

He'd contemplated too long. He waited for the right opportunity, but that didn't come. What came instead was the iron butt plate of a rifle to his stomach. It came swift with brutal force, and he doubled over, gasping for his breath. A second blow with the gun stock, swung down across his back, dropped him to the ground.

While he was down they got his boots off his feet quickly and bound his ankles together so that he couldn't kick, and he couldn't run. In his condition he wouldn't be much for doing anything, anyway. He'd taken some hard blows, and he was in enough pain to render him initially helpless.

He began to feel his wrists aching from the tight rope, and he tasted the blood filling up in his swollen mouth, almost causing him to gag. The frustration he felt was even worse than the physical pain – not being able to do anything about what was happening. A feeling of helplessness he wasn't used to feeling, and it had to be worse than death.

But death was also near. He knew they wouldn't let him live. After what they'd done, they wouldn't be able to. These were cutthroats. Murderous, ruthless thieves. God only knew how many other men fell prey to their wickedness. Now it was his awful turn, and it was a hard thing even to think about.

Suddenly he could feel the anger swell up within him. Angry with himself as much as anything for not being more alert and prepared for these kind of scoundrels. Why hadn't he paid more attention to them back in Sacramento? He had a strong sense then that they were up to no good, and he should have trusted his senses more. And Mr. Thibault warned him to keep his wits about him, that these mountains were home to plenty of outlaws and bad men. He should have expected something like this. Now all he could do was lie down like a sick dog and die – face down in the tall grass while they stripped his camp of all he owned. They'd take the rest of the clothes he wore he was certain, were it not for the blood he'd spilled all over them from his cut lower lip.

He could hear them hurrying to pack up what gear he had, and one of them went off into the trees and returned with their horses. They'd been staked some distance away to prevent horse noises giving away their position. He could hear his own mule braying with a distressing voice. The critter was very much aware of troubles occurring.

"Hurry it up, Clive, let's pack that there miserable mule an' git on outa this draw. Feel somen's a watchin' us frum up thayre on that rock. Don't much like this place."

"I ain't seen no one, you chicken fool! Ain't seen so much's a trace a no one b'sides what this here sorry sucker done left us ta findeem by, bein' he's as green as a three-foot sapplin'."

As much as Nathan hated to admit it, the man had a point. He knew better than to leave a discernible trail. And he'd made too much noise around camp, thinking he was alone in these mountains. But mistakes like these in a wild and lawless land are sure to get a man into trouble. Get him killed. Stupid, all right. Damned stupid. But it was too late for him to correct his mistakes now.

Clive. That was the other one's name. It was a name he would remember. And he would remember the name Leroy. He hadn't known many with those names, so he could remember them. And their faces… He etched the pictures of their faces into his head, so that he wouldn't forget them.

But it appeared that he wouldn't be remembering them for long, because they pulled him off the ground and threw him up onto his mule atop the rest of his gear now bundled together for the trail. And they began to persuade the unwilling beast up the hill by force, toward the rocky outcropping that overlooked the treed and brushy draw and the tiny stream below.

"We'll toss 'im off that rock." Clive explained. "If'n he survives the fall, he kin take up his plight with the powers o' naychur." They laughed hard thinking about it, imagining how unlikely it would be that anyone would ever survive such a drop.

The rock ledge was easily two-hundred feet higher than the shaded area where he'd camped, and possibly even higher than that. And it looked higher from up there than it had from the camp. His mule resisted fiercely, sensing what was going on and not liking any part of it. But they beat the poor creature into compliance, and forced him up to the rock with a struggle.

"We'll take what we kin git fer this miserable beast, soon's we git to Placerville." One of them remarked out of frustration.

This was looking like the end of the line for Nathan. Off that ledge was a long drop, and a steep side of a hill. Tied up like he was, there was not much chance of him breaking the impact of landing. And there was no way to stop it from happening. They were going to pitch him over the edge like discarding a sack of garbage, and he was going to take a fall.

An overwhelming dread swept through his mind. He tried to utter a prayer, that death might be swift, but there wasn't much time for praying.

They pulled him down off the mule and then lifted him up off the ground for the big toss, one holding his ankles and the other holding his head by his ears. It felt as if his ears would be torn free from his head, but the pain from that wasn't what troubled him now. He saw his existence coming to an end within minutes, and that was a sobering thought. He tried to reflect back over his life, but there wasn't much time for reflecting. He saw Emily's face in his mind – thought about how pretty she was, and felt his anger over this happening and that he wouldn't be able to return to her as he'd promised. She'd never know what happened to him. He felt a rage within him, thinking about it.

He'd allowed his mouth to fill with the blood from his lip, and when the closest one holding him up by his ears glanced down at him just before throwing him over the edge, he spit hard into his eyes, causing him to let loose of his end just as they swung Nathan toward the edge.

He felt his back smacking the hard ground beneath him before the one holding his ankles swung his body over the edge, that last-second action almost throwing that one off balance enough to cause him to go over as well. But he apparently grabbed the ledge and pulled himself up while Nathan went on over.

Nathan could hear the loud cursing as he fell free, and then his body jolted with the hard impact, and he saw trees, sky, rocks, weeds, and everything became a blur as he was sliding down the steep hillside over the brush and hard surface. And then he sensed the motion had ended. His falling and sliding had come to a stop, and he felt himself entangled in the vegetation.

Suddenly he couldn't see much of anything but weeds, vines, leaves, and tree branches, and he realized the mass of all that had helped break the last part of his fall. His guess was that it would have been quite a drop from that point if not for the thick brush. He felt suspended there on the steep hillside at the edge of another drop, but it was really difficult to see from where he was, among all of that.

He heard a few faint words spoken up on the rock, but couldn't tell what they were saying, and then it was quiet.

He knew they wouldn't bother coming after him to finish him off, because he was at a tough spot to reach there on a steep slope in thick brush. They might think the fall had already killed him, anyway. And it probably should have, he thought, trying to figure how far he'd fallen.

He didn't move for awhile, or make any noises. He tried to listen over the sound of his breathing, but he didn't hear any more words, or the sounds of horses, or his mule fighting its cruel new masters. He knew they were gone up the trail, leaving him there to die a painfully slow torturous death. He dreaded trying to move, but knew he'd have to try.

Yet he couldn't seem to move much at all. His hands and feet were tied, and his body was in a lot of pain. And he was tangled up something awful in all of those viny weeds. Why hadn't he died quickly? If a man is going to die, it's always better to go quickly. Now he seemed doomed to die slowly, painfully, lingering and moaning like a wounded animal, and he was unable to do much about it. This was going to be a long misery – that helpless feeling that was worse than death.

It occurred to him why the fall didn't kill him quick. His own actions just before he was thrown over the edge had prevented him from being thrown outward as far as intended, resulting in him dropping maybe fifteen or twenty feet to the steep hillside, rather than clearing that to fall a hundred feet or more. And he landed on a glancing impact with the hillside, sliding into a tangle of brush that stopped him there.

Again he felt frustration over his own foolish actions. This all could have been prevented. At every stage he had an opportunity to change the outcome. He could have put that Joslyn into action while it was still in his hand. One of them would likely have killed him right there, but it would have been quick, and it would have all been over by now. And in the process he could have gotten one of them, and stopped at least one from doing this to other unsuspecting, undeserving saps. He surely had a chance, and he blew it. That other way he'd have died like a man, instead of this way, like a miserable dog in the weeds.

He didn't move much at all for awhile. He rested his battered and sore body and tried to think, to assess the predicament he was in. He got to thinking that if he didn't start moving, he'd die right there. It was torture to move, even just to sit up or roll over where he was, but he didn't like the idea of dying there. Remaining in the weeds on the side of a hill was no good. For however long he had left, he should be using the time to try to get to a better place, no matter how much of a struggle it would be. If he could make it to his camp down below, he could die in the cool grass in the shade of those tall trees. That would beat this dry tangled mass of brush up here where the sun baked the hillside most of the day, and the hot rocky ground.

He started to move and immediately felt an excruciating pain shoot through his left side. He wondered if he might have injured his ribs. He was pretty sure it was his left side that came down first on the hard surface, but now his memory of the details concerning his fall was vague. How much could it have mattered to someone so close to death? It was more of a blur to him now.

He stopped to rest again, but an annoying fly buzzed near his blood-matted hair and stirred him back into motion. He struggled to maneuver his body out of the tangle, out into the open where he could find a path down the side.

The heat of the late-morning sun bore down on him once he cleared the thickest part of the brush, and he worked to roll himself to first one side and then the other, worming his way without the aid of free hands or feet.

Without usable limbs he found it a challenge to keep his balance on the steep hill. At one point he slipped, and he found himself sliding over the thorny weeds and rocks a good thirty feet or more, until his body smacked into a small tree that stopped his sliding. He hadn't hit it hard enough to hurt him, but he was already in pain. He might not have noticed much of a difference anyway, if it had. The little tree did prevent him from sliding farther and eventually hitting harder, however, and he was aware of that when he looked down.

The heat from the sun was getting to him by now, and his sweat was stinging his cuts and scrapes. His sore mouth was dry. His struggle to maneuver down the slope was having a draining effect on his energy, and now more than ever he needed his energy.

Again he looked down below him, and it seemed like a long way to the bottom where he wanted to rest in the shade of the trees. There wasn't much shade where he was now, and he realized he would have to really push himself hard to get down there, because it was getting harder to move. He could feel his body stiffening and growing fatigued. Every little movement he attempted was truly an ordeal for him, and a painful ordeal that taxed his reserves of energy that much more. But he found reserves of energy he wasn't sure still existed within him until he called on them. Somehow he was able to keep moving.

Without any warning he felt quickly overcome with dizziness, and he realized he was blacking out. It was a frightening thing to be losing consciousness in such a precarious position. If he started sliding the wrong way, he might not be able to correct it, and the result could be quite hazardous. But his world was fading fast, and he found no strength to hold off the inevitable.

When his eyes opened again to the glaring yellow of sunrays searing his confused senses, he wasn't sure how long he'd been out. His time perception seemed distorted, and the sun was too bright to accurately calculate its position in the sky, at least in his current state of delirium.

Again he felt that dizziness – dizzy from remaining so long under the direct California summer sunlight, and he felt nauseatcd and thought he might vomit any second. He didn't expect to last much longer. At least not there, anyway. He'd have to get himself off that hill pretty soon if he was ever to feel the cool tall grass in the shade again. And so he forced himself into motion once more.

He found that he could aim for a clump of brush, or a tree, and then let himself slide down to that where he could stop and regain himself, and then repeat the process. If he missed his target, he'd fall farther and build up speed enough that the next obstruction would be encountered more abruptly, and when that happened it was unpleasant. But he was able to descend much faster this way, as opposed to trying to crawl and worm his way down slowly, meanwhile consuming the rest of his precious limited supply of energy. Simply letting himself slide required less strength and saved time.

When he was finally able to hear the first sound of the stream below, it gave him an enormously encouraging boost, and he was able to move a little faster. He needed water. His thoughts of ice-cold creek water rushing over rocks were his source of inspiration now, and for the first time since being hauled up to the ledge, he considered the possibility that he might actually have a chance of surviving this ordeal. A slim chance perhaps, considering his multiple injuries, the ropes on his wrists and ankles, and his lack of provisions now in a wild land, but enough of a chance that it was worth fighting for. Any chance was worth fighting for, and even if he died trying he would fight for his life. He realized his struggle was for more than just to survive. This was a struggle to survive so that he could return to Emily.

He knew it wouldn't be a very long time until darkness filled the sky. A matter of hours – he couldn't tell how many. And he wasn't sure he could hold himself together enough to reach his campsite before blacking out again, and losing more time. He felt the day racing by while he moved in slow motion. But darkness would come eventually, and the mountains would cool way down. It had been chilly the night before, all right, but he had his blankets and his fire to keep him warm. The nights would be too cold here for a wounded man without blankets or supplies. This was still June, and he was in a higher elevation here than where he spent his first two nights in the valley.

He tried again to estimate the position of the sun. It appeared high enough that darkness would still be five or six hours away. Right now he was hot, sweating, tired, and thirsty like he'd never been before. That stream couldn't be much farther now.

The blood circulation had been restricted in his wrists now a long while, and his hands were swelling. That rope would have to come off somehow. Without free hands, he wouldn't make it out here. That was becoming ever more evident as he progressed, struggling just to move about.

He had no way to assess his injuries just yet. That would have to wait until later. He couldn't do anything about them right now, anyway. Right now the only thing that seemed at all important was getting to that stream for its fresh cold water, and he knew he'd have to reach it soon if he was going to live much longer.

When he saw the afternoon sunlight glistening off the surface of the stream, he realized it was not far. He could get down to it before it was too late, he was certain, even as drained of energy as his body was now.

Later he was unable to remember how he managed that last twenty or so yards to the stream. Things weren't very clear to him at that point, but somehow he did it, and he would only remember that wet feeling on his sun-baked skin, and the cold creek jolting him to a state of awareness that had previously been thwarted by the trauma of his ordeal.

For the first time in hours he had water to drink, and he began to drink as much as he could, until he felt sick to his stomach and he began vomiting. Too much cold water too fast was a shock to his system.

Not wanting to lose any more fluids from his body, he avoided guzzling any more water, but instead dipped his tired face into the clear running stream and swallowed only small amounts in an effort to gradually hydrate his body.

Even though he felt a little bit sick, or nauseated, the cold water seemed to relieve some of his suffering. And it helped bring him back to life.

Still he knew he was in bad shape. His injuries were plenty serious. And with no doctors within probably twenty miles, his chances for survival were dubious at best, and in the back of his mind he was very much aware of it even if he wouldn't allow himself to admit it. He knew he couldn't allow himself to admit it if he wanted to preserve any hope of living. His survival would now depend largely on his stubbornness – his unwillingness to accept defeat. Without the luxury of favorable odds, a man must compensate with perseverance. It was one of those little bits of advice he used to get from his grandfather now and then. And it always seemed to hold true. He was the wisest man Nathan ever knew, and he'd brought him up to believe in things like that.

He was pretty sure he wouldn't have made it another dismal hour had he not reached the stream. His body had been dehydrating rapidly by then, and he'd lost some blood. But the cooling stream changed a lot of things. The body begins to repair itself when its cells are sufficiently hydrated, and for Nathan, the healing had now begun.

His wrists and ankles were still tightly bound, and that was a serious problem. His fingers were becoming stiff and numb, and they were behind him where he couldn't easily see them. His many attempts to reach the knot in that rope proved futile. And he tried to reach the knots in his ankle ropes, but his sore body just wouldn't bend that far.

He remembered that jackknife he kept under that heavy rock in his camp. Chances were good those men didn't find it. They were too busy gathering up all they could see and in too much of a hurry to search very thoroughly. If Nathan hadn't been face down in the grass he would have noticed whether they found that little cache or not. But that campsite wasn't far from the stream, and not awfully far from where he was now.

The thought of retrieving the jackknife made up another glimmer of hope, because an edge of steel would come as a godsend to anyone in the wilderness without provisions, and Nathan had a very urgent need for a cutting tool. The big problem would be getting the knife open and manipulating its blade to cut through the rope. That knife had a stiff spring holding its blade closed, and with his current lack of dexterity, such a task seemed impossible.

The jackknife wasn't going to be a viable option, he decided. Its chances of doing the job under these circumstances were too slim. Better not to waste precious time and energy on such an uncertain plan as that. The remaining daylight would be better spent inventing a more reliable approach.

The day was wearing on, though, and if those ropes weren't off before nightfall, his situation would be looking extremely grim. In the dark he'd lack the ability to see what he was doing, and this would be challenging enough if he could see. His hands would need the blood circulation now restricted before they would serve again as functional hands, and every minute that passed now made that chance smaller. Without functional hands, a man simply cannot survive alone in the wilderness.

He looked around for a sharp or jagged rock that might suffice as a knife or saw. Back home he'd found his share of flint along the banks of the river, and whenever the flint broke just right it produced sharp edges. He didn't see anything like that here. But across the stream he noticed some large rocks that appeared edgy and possibly abrasive in certain spots. That was going to be his best chance, he thought, knowing it wasn't going to be easy or quick. But a narrow corner of a solid rock might work as a tool to wear through rope fibers, especially when there's a desperate man sawing the rope over that corner – sawing for his life.

His hopeful eyes found the rope cutter he was looking for in those rocks; an angled projection in the rock formation on that hillside looked like a pretty sharp edge from where he was looking. And its height – he thought he should be able to comfortably reach the edge with his arms, and lean back against it while rubbing the rope over it.

Well, it looked possible, anyway. It was still a good forty or more yards away, and he'd have to cross the stream and thick brush to reach it. That would clearly be easy for an average person walking, but how long would it take a tied-up wounded man to crawl? He might be able to hop part of the way, but it would take some work.

After a few minutes of rinsing himself in the refreshing creek, he felt his strength revived enough to start working his way toward the rock. Like a man fighting for his life he pushed himself across every obstacle until he reached it.

With some difficulty he was able to stand upright and lean back against the rock, just as he had planned, and begin to drag the rope up and down over the vertical edge of stone with his weight bearing on it. It was the most awkward operation he could imagine, but he could hear the abrasive narrow corner of stone wearing on the rope's fibers, and he could feel it seem to bite in. He knew it would only be a matter of time until the rope was sawed through.

For the first time in hours he was feeling better than helpless. This was a hard plan, but it was a plan that would ultimately work. Pretty soon, or eventually, his hands would be free. The prospect of it kept him working eagerly, in spite of his now almost crippling pain, to create as much abrasion on the same spot in the rope as his tired and battered body could create.

When he could feel some of the fibers separating, he pressed harder and sawed faster, and even though his body begged him for a rest, he couldn't stop now. The feel of tearing fibers and the weakening of the rope only inspired him to continue in his now frenzied obsession to conquer the tyranny of that binding cable torturing his wrists and hands.

Then suddenly, well before he expected, the hemp broke loose and his hands swung apart, unrestricted. The surprise threw him off balance, and he struggled to regain himself, finding difficulty in believing it at first. But he held his freed hands before his eyes, and stared at them with a new appreciation. They were numb, sore, and swollen, and they were not at all as hands should be, but they were everything to him now.

The next order of business was to get that rope off his ankles. That would be another challenge of its own, because even with his hands now free, his fingers were still weak from their lack of blood for so long. It would take a little time to regain his dexterity in those fingers, and he began to work them, to get the blood flowing again.

With his limp fingers he attempted to untie the knot in the rope. It was too tight. That knot would be a bear even for strong fingers, as tight as it was. And trying to saw that rope over the jagged rock that severed the bindings on his wrists would be especially difficult using his legs, because he wouldn't be able to employ the weight of his body the same way.

But then another idea came to him. If he could find a pointed stick, he might be able to work it through the knot and loosen it up by prying. It would have to be a sturdy little wedge of wood, but there was no shortage of tree branches around.

After pecking at the knot with several twigs, he saw he wasn't getting far with that idea. It still required a degree of finger dexterity, and his sticks kept snapping when he tried to pry with them. He resumed his efforts picking at the knot with his lifeless fingers, hoping to exercise them back to life in the process.

By this time his body was screaming for a rest, and that pain in his side was severe, but his mind was made up. He was going to keep at it until he had that knot untied. He really had no other options. He thought about his jackknife, but it was over at the campsite, and getting its blade open could still be a trick with weak fingers. He was getting some feeling back in those fingers, but he could tell that their strength hadn't yet been fully restored. That would take a bit more time. Fiddling with the knotted rope would seem to be a good way to exercise his fingers, so he continued at it.

Finally after what seemed like an hour (but was likely no more than ten minutes) of picking at the knot, it suddenly began to loosen its hold in the rope, giving Nathan a renewed encouragement that helped him tug and pry at it with invigorated determination.

His fingers seemed to regain quite a bit of strength almost immediately after noticing the knot was giving way, and in another instant his feet were free.

CHAPTER V

It was an enormous relief to have his hands and feet finally free, but he knew that his struggles were far from over. Nightfall wasn't far off, and he could already feel the mountain air cooling as the sun dipped low in the west. It was promising to be a chilly night, and a long one.

Nathan's body was beaten, bruised, damaged to an undetermined degree, exhausted, and hungry. He needed to eat to begin repairing his wounds, but his food was gone. It was taken away with the rest of his supplies. Hunting and foraging could also prove quite difficult for him in his present state.

He recovered his jackknife and flint & steel kit from under the rock where he'd hidden it. He was grateful to have these simple tools. But doing anything with them would require energy, and currently his energy was low. He could not remember a time when he felt as weak and exhausted as he felt right now.

He collapsed onto the bedding of pine boughs he'd collected the day before, and just rested there awhile without moving at all. Freeing his hands and feet and reaching his camp constituted a major achievement for him in his condition, and as much as he needed to eat, he needed to rest. At least for now, resting would have to come first.

As the woods grew darker, the air temperature dropped, and Nathan awoke with chills sometime after the sun had disappeared. The woods seemed completely dark to him by then. The moon, wherever it was up there in the sky, was blocked by tall pines. He found himself in a miserably uncomfortable state; cold, hungry, in pain, and sleepy, though he was unable to sleep like this.

He forced his body to move. He rolled over onto his belly and reached his arms out across the ground, his hands searching for grasses, leaves, pine needles, twigs, dirt, and really any natural debris he could sweep toward him and cover his body with, to insulate himself from the cool night air. And he repeated the process over and over, continuing the effort until he had enough leaves and dirt to bury himself almost completely, maintaining an opening only for his face for breathing and looking straight up into the starry night sky above him.

Before falling back to sleep he realized that he had stopped shivering. If he didn't last until morning, he told himself, at least he would die warm. That alone would make the struggle worth it. Being able to trap his remaining body heat changed things quite a bit. He was actually able to feel a degree of comfort now for the first time in quite awhile. His many other problems would have to wait until morning. For now all he really wanted to do was sleep. And this time he knew it was going to be a long sleep. His body needed it to start the healing process.

It was late into the morning before he awoke to the world around him. The sun had already been up long enough to completely dry away the dew, and the layers of earth and vegetation over his body that had insulated him during the cool of the night were now making him uncomfortably warm. It was a chore to move any part of his body, but he was mighty tired of lying there under all that debris, so he sat up and brushed himself off. He was glad to be alive.

He knew the first thing he needed to do was try to assess his injuries, and check his physical condition. If he had dangerous internal injuries, he should at least have some idea as to what they were, even though he wasn't well educated in medical matters. But if he was generally aware of his injuries, he reasoned, perhaps he could try to avoid doing certain things that might cause further damage. If he had broken ribs, for example, he would want to be careful how he moved, so as to prevent a broken rib from puncturing a lung.

Nearly every part of his body hurt. Judging the full extent of his wounds might be impossible. About the only thing he could be completely certain of was that he had some real injuries, and plenty of them.

He was able to breathe well enough, and he could move his arms and shoulders. That was encouraging. He still felt the pain in his side, but he didn't think he had any broken ribs. Maybe something was cracked in there, but not completely broken. There would be no way for him to know for sure.

With substantial difficulty he stood up on his feet, struggling to keep his balance and straighten his back. His muscles were still just as stiff and sore, if not more so, than they were the previous day.

If he had any broken bones anywhere he didn't know it. He knew he should ask himself things like that, but the question almost got him to laugh. The way his body felt, most of his bones *should* be cracked or broken, though it appeared to him that none actually were, as he found himself currently standing upright on his feet, and his limbs seemed mostly functional. It was encouraging.

When he started feeling a rush of dizziness, he reached for the nearest tree for support. He realized that he wasn't out of the woodpile yet. Recovery was going to be a gradual thing. His pain was excruciating by this time, but he understood the importance of forcing himself up and about. If he didn't overcome this right away, he would just have to keep on trying until he did.

He instinctively glanced up toward the rocky ledge over which he had been tossed, and in the very same instant he was certain he noticed a human silhouette up there quickly pulling back out of sight.

Someone was up there. He hadn't had enough time to see what the person looked like, but someone was up there, and he was being watched. The person obviously did not expect him to glance up when he did, but Nathan knew he could expect him to use more care now in avoiding detection. He wouldn't likely get a second glimpse of the person anytime soon.

Suddenly Nathan's mind was swimming with thoughts and questions. Who was it up there on that ledge? Those same two men who robbed him and left him for dead, maybe? No, it wouldn't likely be them. They'd be long gone by now. If they had come back to finish him off, they'd have already done that. Not likely them. But who, then?

He'd only spotted the silhouette of one person. That didn't mean there couldn't be others up there as well. Only one of them was careless enough to be spotted.

It was most likely an Indian up there. Could be a lone hunter. In the West, white people rarely saw Indians unless the Indians wanted to be seen. At least, that was what Nathan had always heard. This one had slipped up and got discovered. It would be humiliating if he was with a group.

The Indians were different in Missouri. One of Nathan's childhood pals was of Osage heritage, though he'd known a few Shawnee from the government-created Indian Territory. He could always find them whenever he wanted to, because everyone knew where they lived. Things were different here.

Well now he knew that he was being watched by *someone.* He felt uneasy about it, but he realized he should have expected that the regional natives would know all about his existence long before he was aware of theirs. And right now he was completely vulnerable. His health condition was at a low point, and he had no weapons to defend himself with at the present. If the Indians wanted to capture him or take his topknot, they shouldn't have much trouble right now. Possibly they were watching him out of simple curiosity; the entertainment of observing a cruel, lingering white man's death. Certainly they wouldn't have any reason to feel threatened by him. Not now, anyway.

But Nathan was determined to disappoint his audience, if they hoped to watch him die. He would fight for his survival, and live to walk out of these mountains when the time came. If they continued to monitor his progress, they would have something worth watching. He had something to live for now – something greater than all the gold in the Sierra Nevada.

His thoughts about Emily would help him endure his awful pain. He could endure anything, he believed, if it meant seeing her again, and basking again in the glow of her youthful spirit. Everything else seemed almost trivial by comparison.

He realized how fortunate he was to have his folding knife and his flint and steel kit. He had the means to build other tools, weapons, shelter, and fire. He would be able to hunt, make traps, skin animals, and cook the meat he obtained. It would be a challenge all right, but he had the basic tools to work with, and for that he was grateful.

The first tool he decided to fashion was a walking stick. A sturdy pole would be useful to lean on as he limped about in the forest. If it was stout enough, it could also serve as a defensive club, if any critters had thoughts of making a meal out of him.

He began to hobble around in search of a heavy green branch, hunting for the thickest, straightest hardwood branch he could find. He'd be able to cut it from the tree with his knife, by whittling it down at its base and then snapping it off. Something he could finish shaping while he sat around his campfire later. He found a lot of branches that almost met his specifications, but he realized it wasn't going to be the easiest thing to find. Most of the woods he found were too soft.

He found an alder tree he thought looked like it might have some suitable branches, and he saw a green limb that appeared solid enough for his pole. He spent the next half hour or more cutting at it with his knife until the breaking point was narrow enough to snap free. As he whittled the branch down, he thought about how wonderful it was to have functional fingers finally. He could open the knife's blade and grip its handle as well as he ever could, and that was encouraging. In a short amount of time he would have a heavy stick in his hand, and that would help his sense of security out here.

In spite of his condition, he remained active throughout the day, and by nightfall he had some accomplishments to feel good about. He had a lean-to shelter set up by interweaving pine boughs for the walls and roof, and he'd made a comfortable fire after collecting a supply of dead wood to burn through the night.

The only foods he was yet able to find were thimble berries, blue elderberries, and miner's lettuce. He recognized them from sketches he'd seen in a nature book, and he wondered how many more varieties of edible plants existed around him and along the stream that he didn't recognize. But as glad as he was to have anything at all to eat, it still wasn't enough. He was fiercely hungry. He realized he needed meat, and he realized he'd be lucky to get any meat anytime soon. Hunting, fishing, and building traps all took time and energy. That would all have to wait until the following day at any rate, when there would be light enough to see.

He had gathered a sizeable pile of pine boughs besides what he used to build his shelter with, and he slept on some and covered most of his body with the rest inside his lean-to. This was promising to be a more comfortable night than the one before, because of all the effort he'd invested to improve his situation. His body was healing slowly, but he knew he still had a ways to go.

He was exhausted from the day, and he fell asleep easily. The last thing he remembered before falling asleep was the gentle crackling of tiny flames. His campfire died out slowly while he slept.

When morning came, he found it more difficult to move than ever before. His body just didn't want to start. He had to force himself up out from his cocoon of pine branches.

He pulled himself up onto his feet, with the help of the thick walking stick he'd made. It was a real struggle for him, just to stand upright. It seemed harder than the day before, and he worried that his condition might be worsening, rather than improving.

Now he looked around for a forked stick. He realized he needed a crutch more than a straight walking stick. He needed something he could lean his weight upon, while he made his way about. He'd have to be able to get about if he was going to survive, and it was currently rather difficult to do. But a hunter has to be mobile.

He wondered if the fish were worth catching in that small stream. He would be able to whittle wooden fishhooks with his knife, as he had previously planned to do, but he wasn't sure what he would use for string now to tie them to. Indians knew how to make string from tree bark, but he didn't know how they did it. Perhaps he could experiment and figure it out.

And he would have to search for bait. Earthworms, large insects, or grubs – he would search for whatever he could find. A digging stick would be a handy tool for that, and he could whittle one from a tree branch with his knife.

His mind was swimming with problem-solving ideas. He knew that the only way he would have any chance of making it would be to keep working at improving his situation, in spite of whatever physical setbacks he faced. He was thoroughly convinced that, if at any time he chose to give up the fight, it would mean never seeing Emily again. He couldn't consider that as an option. Every struggle he struggled, no matter how unpleasant, provided at least a chance to survive – survive to get back to Emily, and lose himself in her embrace once again. The very thought of it made him forget all about his battered sore body, and his painfully empty stomach, if only for a short while.

And he started getting busy. He started limping around the immediate area surrounding his camp, and looking closely at everything he saw, asking himself how each thing might be useful. He saw rocks as hammers, as anvils, as projectiles to throw if needed in an emergency of self-defense. He saw sticks as digging tools and other useful implements, as well as a fuel source for his campfire. Suddenly he was seeing everything differently than he ever had before. He was thinking how he might build all the things he needed in his new environment, using whatever he could find. His mind was working like a steam engine.

His need for meat got him to thinking about how he might build an animal trap. Strands from the short rope sections might work as snare cord, but a big heavy rock propped up by some kind of trigger arrangement, with notched sticks maybe, along a path used by small mammals or birds might serve easily as a deadfall. If he set several such deadfalls, his chance for success would be greatly increased. He had never had any desire to trap animals before now, thinking it a rather cruel activity, but right now he was desperately hungry. The cruelty of trapping animals seemed insignificant at the moment, and he made his way through the woods searching for animal trails, dens, or any sign of wildlife. He was determined to capture meat.

He also found a long Y-shaped branch and cut it into a crude crutch. It was easier to get around once he had his crutch to lean on. But he couldn't stop thinking about how to build traps. He was feeling weaker and weaker from his lack of nutrition. All these chores required energy, and his body required a lot more fuel than a few bites of wild greens and some berries. He was getting noticeably shaky and his headache became almost incapacitating. He would need to eat something substantial pretty soon, and he knew it.

But immediate relief was not in sight. The only idea he had at the moment was to make his way down to the water and drink as much as he could drink. Water in his body was a whole lot better than nothing, he told himself, and he started for the stream. The trip was a lot easier now with the crutch stick to lean on.

The Indians were watching him. He could feel the intensity of their observing eyes, monitoring his every move. He wondered how many of them were there. He thought it felt like the eyes of half a dozen observers, but he had no way to count them.

They watched him, waiting to see how long it takes for a white man in his situation to succumb to the ravages of this mountainous environment. Nature could be unforgiving. It provided no doctors, nor instructions as to how to obtain the necessities of survival.

Nathan believed he knew what was going through the minds of his observers, and he was going to show them one white man who wouldn't be beaten. Suddenly his torturing hunger seemed less gripping. Suddenly, after guzzling some cold stream water, he found the strength he would need to function. He thought about certain tasks that would have to be accomplished, and he started getting to work. Those Indians would see a white man who wasn't totally helpless.

He found deadfall traps the easiest to build, because they didn't require any digging into the rocky earth, or any particularly intricate components. Nor was string required in their construction. He simply notched some sticks to comprise the supports and trigger release, and propped up a heavy rock, or in some cases a large log in position across the path of small animals, and left it alone. He set a number of such traps before moving on to the next order of business.

Through experimentation he was able to assemble a fish trap using strands from his ankle ropes to tie the ends of branches together. He used a basket weave method of interlocking the thin branches into a funnel-shaped cage, with an inverted one-way entrance.

He then piled rocks up in the stream in such a way as to create a narrow passage from one pool to another, and placed his makeshift fish trap in the end of the runnel he'd created, holding it down wedged under a tough springy protruding tree root.

All of these efforts took time, but it takes quite awhile for a man to starve to death. If he made proper use of his time, he should have enough. He would keep busy improving his living conditions.

It was the accomplishment of even the most basic of chores that lifted his morale above the realization of his desperation. These things; his shelter, campfire, walking tools, and traps, all gave him something to feel good about. For if he could build them while in his current condition, what else might he be capable of? He began to stop doubting his survivability. His body would heal, he told himself, if he kept his mind focused on overcoming the struggles of his predicament.

And of course, now he had an audience. His activities were monitored by the curious eyes of mountain natives, and as primitive as these people were in his mind, he also understood that they were expert woodsmen. If for no other reason now, Nathan's pride would not let him fail.

He planned to check his traps every few hours, but he didn't expect to have a catch for awhile. He was aware that it takes time for the human scent to dissipate. He expected to have his best luck with the fish trap in the stream. He thought he should check on that about every hour during daylight.

But his body's nutritional requirements were too urgent to bide even another hour more without him collapsing, the way he felt, and while scouting up some firewood he discovered a cluster of various bugs and grubs under a fallen dead tree. Without contemplating this find long enough to talk himself out of it, he scooped up all he could with both hands and shoved them into his mouth, chewing and swallowing quickly.

He surprised himself by not gagging, and he decided to search for more. Though it wasn't exactly what he was used to eating, it was food all right. Bugs and worms could sustain him, and they were easy to catch. He would eat as many crawly creatures as he could lay his hands on, if it meant avoiding starvation. At least until he had more familiar meat caught in one of his traps, he would eat what he could find, and be grateful for it.

He knew that keeping himself busy would be to his benefit. It was one thing completely within his control. If he was awake and could move, he could remain active. He could continuously work to improve his situation, and he reminded himself of that again and again. If he were to quit working at things, his muscles would grow stiff, his mind would wane, and his motivation would disappear. The only time he would stop would be when he needed a rest, and his resting periods would have to be limited. There was a lot of work to do.

His activities were exhausting, but also inspiring. Before the day had passed, he had improved his shelter, collected enough sticks of firewood to burn for several days, retrieved a squirrel from one of his traps and two stream fish from his fish trap, assembled a very basic but useful array of stone and wooden tools, and he had woven two basket containers. One was to carry various tools and raw materials in, and the other to store nuts, berries, greens, and whatever he could find to eat.

Things were truly starting to look up, he was thinking as squirrel meat on a green stick smoked over flickering flames, and two gutted trout lay baking on hot rocks lining his campfire.

His clothing, what he still wore of it, was torn and stained, but the aroma of wood smoke and cooking meat overruled the stale smells of dried blood mixed with dirt and sweat. He was currently without a coat, or a hat, or shoes of any kind, but he had a warm fire, a good shelter, and meat. Most of his body still ached, but he didn't want to think about that right now. Tonight he wouldn't be going to bed on an empty stomach, and things were looking up.

He was focused on how tasty that last trout was when he heard a rustling in the brush off to his right. He turned to look just as a black bear showed itself, and approached his camp indirectly, apparently trying to size up what Nathan was, and where the food might be located.

Nathan watched cautiously as the bear ambled slowly towards him. He finished chewing his last two bites quickly and swallowed, so as to leave no precious meat for this intruder. The bear showed his teeth and waved his nose back and forth several times, and Nathan didn't move.

While they stared at each other, seconds seemed like minutes, and Nathan could feel his heart beating loudly in his chest. He watched the bear's moves closely, trying to judge what he would do next, and sense his thought process. The bear came around because of the smell of cooking meat, but the meat had now been eaten. Maybe the bear would be angered over this disappointment and become unmanageable. There was no way to know what it would do. It remained twenty feet away, making intimidating gestures.

Nathan's left hand slowly found the long stick he'd been using to stir the fire, and he held the end of it directly over the flames as his eyes stayed locked on this beast in front of him, waiting for it to make a move. By not making any sudden movements himself, he avoided accelerating the probably inevitable confrontation, to which the bear held the obvious advantage.

And then the bear made an aggressive advance. The burning stick in Nathan's hand was instinctively raised from the fire and pointed in the direction of the furry monster, and when the bear was close enough to feel the flames being shoved toward its face it slowed its approach and eventually backed off. It could easily have knocked the flaming stick out of Nathan's hand, but it clearly didn't like the fire, and it apparently decided that it didn't want to mess with something like that. Fire was something the bear didn't completely understand.

The bear remained for a few minutes, looked about Nathan's camp, and then seemed to lose interest in the whole matter. It turned around and left the area, leaving Nathan awestruck, and noticeably relieved. He took a deep breath and sat back down near his fire, extending his hands over the flames and smoke to dry away the nervous sweat.

His encounter with the bear seemed to put him on edge well into the night. He kept his fire stoked, and he stared into the flames for hours. His physical exhaustion and drowsiness were soon competing with his paranoia, for when darkness came he couldn't see beyond the shadow of his shelter, which danced in concert with the flickering flames that provided his only light. He felt uncomfortably vulnerable anywhere except close to the fire.

The question he couldn't stop asking was would the beast return, maybe hoping to catch him off guard in the darkness after the fire was out? He knew he'd have a hard time trying to defend his camp in the dark, but at the same time he wasn't sure he'd be able to keep the fire burning until first light. And the heavier his eyelids felt, the greater his dilemma.

Finally his need for rest won out, and he abandoned the warmth of the hot coals for the cover of his shelter, and the springy bed of pine boughs, into which he crawled for the remainder of the night and eventually fell asleep. But it was a night of fitful rest, and limited sleep. The air had cooled, and thunderclouds rumbled as morning approached. Before any sign of sunlight showed itself, cold raindrops were falling through the trees overhead, wetting down the forest in all directions.

This unexpected precipitation tapered off from what seemed like maybe ten minutes of a torrential downpour to a more gentle drizzle, which persisted for better than an hour before the next heavy drenching came, thoroughly saturating the whole environment.

Nathan hadn't planned on a rainstorm. His shelter, while basically sturdy enough and well constructed to shed most of the water with its layers of interwoven branches, wasn't built with heavy showers in mind. This was June. It was supposed to be the dry season. His shelter was intended more as a windbreak, and really a psychological fortress against the elements. Trickles of moisture eventually found their way through the pine boughs, but the main torrents rolled off, and Nathan was mighty glad to have made the effort getting it put up.

Daylight came without even a glimpse of the sun. Gray clouds hung in tight between the mountains, and the air was a damp cold fog. Occasionally the sky would sprinkle water over the trees, and a drop would fall through the branches. Everything outside the shelter appeared wet, and the question he began to ask himself was how long will this last?

These new weather conditions would make it difficult to get the fire going, and to keep himself dry and warm. The animals, most of them, would also be seeking shelter and burrowing deeper into their dens, making his hunting and trapping possibly less productive, at least for awhile.

When he moved he realized his physical energy was substantially below normal. That seemed strange after a night of rest. He should not still be tired from yesterday's activities. When he exited the little opening to his tiny hut, he stood up and walked about. The wet grass felt cold on his bare feet, and his tattered trousers picked up moisture from the brushy vegetation he walked through. Wet pants. That's a cold feeling. He'd want to dry them over the fire, but he'd have to get the fire lighted first, and that could be tough. Every piece of wood he touched was soaking wet. There was nothing around dry enough to burn. Even his tinder had become damp from the moisture in the air.

He felt chilled, and he felt weak. This was not encouraging. The dampness wouldn't be around forever, and when the sun returned, there would be a lot of work to do. But at the moment he lacked the energy to do much of anything. He thought about trying to light the fire, but it didn't look like a practical option at the moment. About the only thing he really wanted to do was crawl back into his hole and rest a little longer, and maybe reserve his energy until conditions were more suitable for getting out and about.

Nothing in the whole world seemed as important as getting some sleep. He didn't even feel hungry, in spite of his awareness of his nutritional needs. He crawled back into his shelter and buried himself under heaps of pine boughs, trying to get warm. It was the driest place in the forest, he was certain, but even in there he could feel the dampness.

He was exhausted, and chilled, but he didn't know what his problem was. He didn't feel entirely well, but he wasn't entirely miserable, either. He simply had almost no energy in his body, and he wanted to escape the conscious world, and do nothing at all but sleep.

Another volley of raindrops could be heard pelting the roof of pine needles over his head, and his sense was that the rain was going to continue off and on for awhile, maybe all day or longer, and the woods weren't going to be drying out anytime soon.

But his sense of urgency – his passion to get things done, had vanished. Finding food, watching out for dangerous beasts like the bear, building tools, gathering firewood… Nothing seemed imperative right now. Even the very reason he came to these mountains – to find gold, even that seemed insufficiently important to coax him out of his den.

He felt the chills sweep over his body, and he realized he'd been shivering. He couldn't seem to find warmth no matter how much insulation he surrounded his body in, and he felt too weak to get up and attempt to build a fire.

His mind had trailed off into a dream and then abruptly he was awake again, only this time his face felt hot, and then his whole body felt hot, like he was on fire. Instead of that cold damp misery, his body now felt suffocated by the mound of pine boughs he'd burrowed into, and he lifted the heap off of himself with the limited amount of strength he could muster. It felt heavy to him. By now he was sweating profusely, and he felt a desperate need to get himself out into the open air where he could breathe.

He worked his way out of his shelter where he hoped the air might cool him down. The rain had diminished to just a light drizzle, hardly more than a mist, but Nathan was nearly oblivious to it.

His struggle to escape the confines of his shelter had him crawling on the ground, and he continued crawling at almost the pace of a snail. He seemed convinced that while his body was moving he would be avoiding any mental focus on his state of discomfort. Crawling engaged his body and his mind, and required a degree of mental concentration, so he continued crawling along the ground, through the wet grass and weeds.

He wasn't able to keep himself awake very well at all. He kept finding himself waking up from bizarre dreams, one after another, until he became confused as to when he was having a dream, and when he was awake. Everything eventually seemed to blend into a fuzzy hallucination.

At one point he dreamt he was talking to the old hermit he'd heard about, who wore the patch over his eye. It was as strange a dream as any he could remember. He dreamt that the old man had lifted him up onto a makeshift travois and began to drag him away. He tried to ask him where he was taking him, but his words came out as incomprehensible mumbling. He simply felt too tired to articulate the simplest phrases, too tired even in his state of delirium. But he knew this had to be a dream, because if he'd been awake, he'd have anxiously asked the old man where he could find some gold. After all, that was the main reason he was here. His subconscious created this dream about seeing the old man, because he was here for the gold. Crazy, all right. His mind was playing cruel tricks on him.

CHAPTER VI

Nathan awoke amidst unfamiliar surroundings. It was somewhat of a dingy atmosphere. He found himself lying on a bunk consisting of a frame of pine logs lashed together, with strips of rawhide strung across the center upon which rested a cushion of wool blankets.

The earthen inner walls of this dwelling were braced by hardwood timbers wedged into their position in such a way as to hold back the earth from collapsing into the cave-like chamber.

At one end was a stone and clay fireplace whose chimney was apparently nothing more than a funnel-shaped hole bored straight up through the ground of what would seem to be a hillside. Built into this fireplace was a traditional swinging pothook upon which hung a large cast iron pot.

On both sides of the fireplace clusters of miscellaneous tools were leaned against the wall, including axes, shovels, picks, sledge hammers, a broom, dust pan, and even a cavalry saber in a scabbard.

At the other end of the room was a stout entrance door built of thick planks hinged to a heavy frame of timbers. And the walls – the timbers that held back the earth, were decorated with animal skins, iron traps, snowshoes, frying pans, powder horns, and three rifles; two caplock and one with flint ignition, hung on protruding pegs, the gun barrels spanning across two vertical timbers on one wall, and two huge caplock horse pistols hung by their trigger guards on pegs into the opposite wall. Jars, tin cans, and other supplies rested on simple shelving, along with perhaps two dozen books. The floor of the room looked like creek gravel packed down hard.

There was a rough-hewn wooden table in the middle of the room, upon which rested an oil lamp, a tall wooden mug, and one of Colt's Dragoon six-shooters.

Seated at this table across facing Nathan with one hand over the Dragoon and his one good eye monitoring Nathan closely, was an older fellow with a white beard, a seasoned face, and a dark leather patch over one eye. He wore crudely sewn buckskin attire.

"What is this place?" Nathan asked, looking up at the dark ceiling above him, realizing it was probably dirt and rocks held up by the planks spanning the heavy timbers. "Some kind of cellar, maybe?"

"I'd say that's a fair observation." Explained the one-eyed mountain man. "If a man intends to live in these parts a long time, such as I have, he needs accommodations more permanent than either a canvas tent or a thatched hut, but not so visible as a wooden house. I spent nearly two years digging this cave and building the sturdy framework that prevents it from caving in, but I'd say it was worth the effort."

Nathan's wandering eyes swept across the dim space, illuminated only by the oil lamp on the table.

"Impressive, all right." He remarked "As far as I'm concerned, it's no less than a grand hotel. But why am I here?"

"Forgive me for interfering with your camping experience, young man. I don't normally mettle in the affairs of other woodsmen. But it didn't look like you were doing so well. It didn't look like you'd make it another night out there in the elements. You seemed to be running a powerful high fever."

"Well I owe you then, sir. But why would you be so concerned about a stranger like myself?"

The bearded old man stared at the wooden mug in front of him, cupping his hands around it, and paused in serious thought before speaking.

"Because... well, I was in a similar situation once, and someone built a travois and carried me away to a warm, dry shelter. I'd have died for certain if... Well anyway, I've had a debt to repay for a long, long time."

"Certainly now I have a debt to repay." Nathan acknowledged, sitting upright on the edge of the bunk slowly. He still felt physically weak, but his fever was gone.

"How long was I asleep?"

"Two days. Well, closer to three days if you count your sleep in camp before I arrived."

"Three days?!? That's a mighty long time to be sleeping. Don't think I've ever slept that long before. How did you know about me, and that I was not well, anyway?"

"Panpakan hunters sent one from their village to inform me. They were keeping a close watch on you. That's a common thing here. I catch 'em spying on me now and again, too. It's just their way. But they remembered that I had a debt, and they sent for me, so I could pay back my debt. Now I'm square with the world." He raised his mug to his lips and gulped once, then planted the mug firmly on the table. He had a satisfied look of achievement in his eyes.

"But I don't understand." Nathan said. "Wouldn't you owe your debt only to the individual who helped you?"

"Well now, there's a thing you need to know about these people. That individual, who was a scout from a village two days south, died from a bad infection a short time later, so I never had a chance to pay him back. What's important to know about these people is how they think – their customs and traditions. You see, in their way of thinking, if you owe a debt to someone, it doesn't die with that person. If the person dies before you settle your score, you still owe the debt until you account for it in like manner, some way or another."

Nathan nodded. He never thought about it before, but it kind of made sense, at least the way this old man was telling it. But now he was the one who would have to live under the burden of obligation, until he could find some way to pay the old man back.

"Well now I've got a debt to pay myself, all right." Nathan acknowledged. "You're that old timer I heard about, who knows where to find gold, aren't you? That was the whole reason I came up here, to find gold."

The old man shook his head in disgust, then grumbled. "The reason most of us wind up here, that's a fact, but no good ever comes of it. Just look at yourself now. Thought you'd get rich, right? But you don't even have any shoes! And you damn near died of exposure. Just look where the lust for shiny yellow gold has taken you."

"Wasn't my prospecting that pitched me over that big rock, or stole my shoes and my mule and my Ballard rifle. None of that had anything to do with gold. I was jumped and robbed when I had no gold at all."

"Except for the fact you'd probably never been up here crossing paths with them that did that to you, were it not for the lure of gold."

"But you know where to find it. They told me you know where to find it, and I intend to find it. It's why I'm here."

Just then the old man got up from the table and went to the fireplace. He lifted two clay bowls from a stack and took a ladle off a hook, and then swung the iron pot off the fire, dipping a tiny sample of its contents out for his personal taste inspection. With a nod of approval, he proceeded to fill the two bowls.

Immediately Nathan's sense of smell returned to him, and he perceived the pleasing aroma of cooked stew. He could feel himself tremble at the prospect of a warm hearty meal.

"You won't have much need for gold or anything else if you don't get some proper food in your belly pretty quick." The old man said while setting the two full bowls on the table.

"Sure smells good, whatever it is."

"It's my own formula; chunks of carrots, potatoes, wild onions, and rattlesnake meat. Sometimes I throw in venison, too, but this happens to be the wrong time of year for venison. I grow my own vegetables. I have a garden. If you're up to sitting at the table, a bowl of this might do you some good."

Nathan managed to get himself into a chair at the table, which wasn't as easy a task as he thought it would be. A full bowl of steaming stew was set in front of him, making the effort well worth it.

He ate slowly at first, knowing that a substantial meal like this would be a shock to his system. But he had to keep himself disciplined. He was hungry enough to devour the bowl's entire contents in a matter of seconds.

He chewed slowly and swallowed. "You are the one they told me about, aren't you? You're the old timer who's taken bags full of gold into Sacramento."

"I've found a few good nuggets over the years. That's a fact. And I suppose you could say I'm an old timer. I'll turn eighty this spring. But my legal name is Milton Franklin Galley."

Nathan scooped another spoonful into his mouth and chewed slowly, watching Milton while he ate. The old man appeared to fully enjoy his stew, which wasn't any wonder. It had excellent flavor.

"Well I don't know why they told me you're unfriendly. You don't seem that way to me."

Milton swallowed, then pondered on this bit of gossip for a moment before bursting into laughter.

"What is your name, young man?" He asked after his chuckling subsided.

"I'm sorry. My name is Nathan Clayburn."

"Where are you from, Nathan?"

"Missouri."

"I might've guessed it. I've been to St. Louis myself. But now I'll tell you something about those city folks there in Sacramento. Most of 'em spend their whole lives as slaves to others for the purpose of gaining capital. You could say they're enslaved by money, or their need for money. Perhaps it's not so bad, really. Keeps businesses running, and gives some folks a sense of purpose. But it's their way of life, not mine.

"I don't want to be a slave to their system. So I try not to get too friendly with those folks in the cities. I have all the resources I need right here in these mountains. If I need supplies, I can purchase all I need with the gold I harvest from these streams."

"Same as I aim to do."

"You need a spell of recovery before you go searching the streams."

"Well I'm feeling better already, thanks to your stew. I sure do owe you a lot. I figure I'd be dead by now if…"

"If you rush things, you'll kill yourself anyway. Get yourself recovered, and I'll show you how to find some gold. And I know where a great treasure is hidden. Help me fetch it, and I'll split it with you. But you have to get healthy first. It will take a lot of work."

This mention of a treasure intrigued Nathan. His eyes widened, and his spoon stopped above the bowl before him.

"Treasure? You mean like giant nuggets?"

"I mean like a Spanish treasure cached along the coast more than two-hundred years ago. I've spent years researching the whole thing, and I believe I know where it is, but I can't get it by myself."

"The coast," Nathan noted "that's quite a stretch from here. What about transportation? Unfortunately I lost my mule. But a couple horses, maybe three horses, or four horses, and lots of supplies. We'd need lots of supplies. Pack saddles, guns, tools, provisions…"

"Slow down there, young man. We can work all that out. We'll get the supplies and horses we need. But you need to finish your stew. Get yourself healthy. That's what you need to take care of right now."

Nathan resumed his eating, now consumed with the thought of hunting a larger treasure than he had previously envisioned. He was almost in a trance, though he continued spooning out stew and eating it slowly.

Tree squirrels were making quite a racket of chattering by the time the sun had warmed the morning woods for an hour. Nathan felt pretty good now, and most of his prior strength had returned. His wounds were well along in their healing.

He and Milton worked together sawing and splitting firewood outside the cave door, which faced a saddle of slightly over two hundred feet bridging two hills. Milton's front yard, if it could be likened to such, much resembled the ridge between knuckles on a hand. There was an area in the middle which was mostly level, and the old man had thinned the trees there. His garden was off to one side, and several scattered stumps served as supports for rusty iron tools; a box vise mounted on one, and an anvil on another. This area was his outdoor workshop.

The place was on relatively high ground, outside the regular pathways of any white men. The local natives were all acquainted with Milton Galley and his cave, and both he and they lived in mutual respect of one another. They knew he was never a threat to them or their way of life, and they left him alone for the most part.

Nathan learned that Milton's cave was almost two miles from where he had camped, and he was in awe of the feat the old timer achieved by dragging him up here on the travois. That would be a chore for any man, he imagined, and certainly a struggle for someone up in his years the way Milton was. But this old timer wasn't much at all like others Nathan had known. In some respects, Milton was something of a mystery, possessing a mixture of contradictions.

He was a man of small frame and stature, showing his years on his face and at times appearing almost frail, yet again and again he demonstrated the physical strength and stamina of an athlete less than half his age.

His educational background was another mystery. Eventually Nathan noticed his extraordinary ability to articulate things, and his recollection of classical literature was obviously extensive. He would occasionally recite poetry or quote lengthy passages from books. Milton might have had the look of a simpleton, but in actuality he was a well-educated man. He may well have been self-educated for all Nathan knew, but he was learned nevertheless. And his level of intelligence was impressive to Nathan. At times the old timer seemed a lot like his own grandfather, displaying many of the same qualities.

Milton stood a small round upon one of the tree stumps and aligned his splitter maul precisely where he wanted the log to split before raising it for the full swing. The head of the maul came down swiftly and exactly where he intended, and the two half logs flew several yards in opposite directions.

As if ignoring the old timer's satisfying chop, Nathan imitated the activity with a round of pine on a different stump and a second maul, similarly changing one log into two half logs. The element of competition kept both mauls swinging progressively and steadily faster.

The two men continued their work for an hour or more, chopping, splitting, sizing down the sawed logs and then stacking them outside the cave door, ready for the fireplace.

"We're going to need more gold." Milton explained, taking a break from chopping and wiping the sweat off his forehead with a rag. "I've collected a few good nuggets, but they won't be enough to buy what we'll need."

"Well, that's a whole lot better than I've done." Nathan responded. "I panned that crick near my camp right after I arrived. I never found so much as a flake."

The old timer shook his head. "That stream never did pay well, as far as I know. I panned it myself at least a dozen times over the years. In fact, I've panned just about every stream I've come across in these mountains. But I know a place not far from the cave where I've always done well. If we work it hard enough, we should harvest enough in a week to outfit ourselves in fine style."

Nathan leaned his maul against the stump. "I'm ready to give it a try right now." He said.

Milton had several old rusty gold pans he'd used for years, plus a rocker with a sloping board of ridges to trap gold washed through the contraption. Within a half-hour they were at the stream beginning their work. The old timer knew from experience that it would be hard slow work, but it would be consistent, and it would yield good rewards.

He watched Nathan slosh water and sand around and around in his pan without recovering so much as a pinhead speck of gold.

"Now look here, young man, that yellow metal is some heavy kind of matter. It'll drop directly into the ridge of your pan. No need to roll the gravel around twenty times. You don't need to worry about washing the gold away. It'll drop right through. Look, here's how you get to it quick."

Milton plopped a fistful of mud into his own pan from a carefully selected location, dipped it into the stream, and swished it back and forth vigorously a few times until the majority of the material had washed out with the current. Then he removed a pair of eyeglasses with one good lens from his buckskin pouch and placed them on his face to aid his inspection of what remained in his pan. A quick glance confirmed his expectation. He handed his pan to Nathan.

"See all that yellow there?"

Three nuggets, each almost the size of a grain of rice glimmered in the sunlight, appearing much larger than their actual size.

"Yes. That's amazing!" Nathan said, peering close into the pan. "But how can I do that?"

"Just like I showed you. You won't get color like that every time, but this stream is exceptionally good. You should come up with something good most of the time. Don't be afraid the gold will float away. It sinks fast. It won't float away."

Nathan followed Milton's instructions with his next try, and discovered two very tiny nuggets after sloshing away the bulk of the material out of his pan. He was thrilled with this first bit of success, and began working more aggressively. Those tiny nuggets might as well have been mountains of gold.

Their work continued through the rest of the week, tramping about in the cold stream and exploring the different tributaries that fed it, panning material from its banks as well as from its bed rocks, and running dirt from neighboring hillsides through the rocker with buckets of stream water. Some sites yielded more than others, as was usual. Milton never ran out of new ideas to try.

Some days were predictably more productive than others, but between the two of them they'd collected a good batch of nuggets before the week had passed, several of which were impressive in size. It was the most productive stream the old timer had ever worked, and it would be some time before it would be panned out. That was apparent. But he'd been working it off and on for several years. Even when other streams in the region seemed to dry up on nuggets, this one remained faithful. There was more gold to find in and around it than he could ever find in three lifetimes, he was convinced. But as reliable as it was, it wasn't easy money by any means. Even here, a man had to work hard for what he found. Milton never bothered to stake a claim.

"We've got nearly five pounds mostly pure gold between the two of us now, and that will buy us a proper outfit for this expedition." Milton announced after weighing the last batch on his balance scale.

The rest of the evening was spent sitting around the fireplace sipping rum and drawing up a list of supplies they would be shopping for and planning the details of their journey. Nathan had never acquired much of a taste for liquor, but he admitted to himself that he was enjoying this.

"First thing I'm buying is a new pair of boots." Nathan said, expressing his eagerness to protect his feet, which had grown noticeably tougher over the last few weeks. "Sure tired of running around with bare feet all over the place."

"You'll be a cripple whilst you break new boots in, but they're better than bare feet. That's a sure bet. As for me, the elk moccasins I made myself serve just fine. I'd learned to keep them in a stirrup well enough last time I did any riding, and they allow more flexibility. I may never wear hard-soled boots again."

"Second thing I want is a shave and a haircut." Nathan added, imagining their trip back to the civilized world. "And maybe a warm bath. Is Sacramento on our route?"

"Yes, and we'll want to outfit there. Our first stop should be Placerville, though. We should get our horses there if we can. Sacramento will be a better place for acquiring the bulk of our gear, but it's a hell of a long walk to Sacramento. I've done it many times."

Just then Milton unrolled a two-foot square of paper and spread it out on his table, and suspended a lantern where its light shone on most of the paper.

Nathan could see that it was a hand-sketched map cluttered with extensive notations, and its markings were difficult to read in certain areas where they were slightly faded or where the paper had been wrinkled or torn.

"I've been constructing my own treasure map for a long time," Milton explained "based on many years of research." He pointed to a bookshelf full of books. "More than half of those books I've collected are history books, mainly focusing on California's history."

"Did you read about this treasure in books?"

Milton shook his head. "There's more to this story than you'll find in any book. If it were that simple, I'm certain the treasure would be long gone by now. But I don't believe it is. No, the truth is, I first heard about it from Yuki Indians. That was thirteen years ago."

"I don't understand." Nathan said "If the Indians knew about it, why wouldn't they claim it for themselves?"

"According to their story, they tried. But they couldn't recover it because they didn't have the proper tools. There is supposed to be a massive stone, a bolder if you will, covering the top of two large chests. An iron anchor wedged into the walls of the hole prevent the weight of the stone from crushing the chests, supposedly. Anyone endeavoring to access the treasure must first remove that huge rock and that anchor from a deep narrow hole in the rocks on a treacherous cliff along the ocean. The natives claim to have tried but failed. I'm not altogether sure the tale is believed by the new generation of natives who tell it, or if they do, why they don't simply obtain the necessary equipment to expose the cache. Perhaps the story itself is more valued by them than the material riches contained therein. I really can't speak for them on that. Who can ever say what goes through their heads? But I have thought about it a long time, and I've come up with some ideas for prying up the rock, and then lifting out the anchor and the two chests. We'll need some large steel hooks, some carbon steel drill bits, heavy ropes and blocks and tackles. We'll need a cross cut saw, hammers, axe, pry bars, and other tools as well, which can be purchased in Sacramento. I'll add these items to our shopping list, everything we'll need to construct a small framework of timbers over the hole, sturdy enough to support the weight of the chests. We'll erect the structure at the site."

"This sounds like a major endeavor, all right." Nathan noted. "But you're sure the treasure's there? You wouldn't go to this extent unless you were sure, would you?"

Milton paused to consider the question. "No." He replied. "I'm not *absolutely* sure about anything. I scouted the coast last spring, and I believe I've found the hole where the chests are, *if* they are indeed there. But to me it's worth the effort. I believe the chests are there.

"In my research I spent nearly five years corresponding with government record keepers of Spain, of Mexico, of the State of California, as well as with numerous museums hoping to find pieces of this puzzle in hidden archives somewhere, but official records make no reference to treasures or cargoes being cached along the California coast."

"The Indian story must have sounded credible to you, then."

Milton shook his head. "No, it didn't. Not when I first heard it. It sounded like a wild fantasy. Most natives I've known had a very creative imagination. And I'd read everything I could find about ships sailing up and down the coast, but found nothing about treasures or treasure ships in the Pacific.

"According to the story, a great sailing vessel landed near Cape Mendocino and cached some of her cargo; two large trunks and something else made of iron, in the rocky cliffs. But important details such as the exact spot where the cargo was cached were left out. And the Indians had no idea as to what the cargo consisted of, or why it was put there. They apparently observed this event from a distance, undetected by the ship's crew."

"You said you believe it was a Spanish ship."

"Yes, that's correct. Determining the time period when this was to have occurred was my next challenge. The natives don't write things down, so a concise record wasn't available. But the description of the vessel suggested a Spanish galleon, and counting the generations back to those original witnesses gave me a rough estimate of somewhere between 1580 to 1640. I had to conduct a number of interviews, which cost me nearly five gallons of whiskey. But most of the Indians I spoke to can name their chiefs going back several hundred years, and it's one of their systems for keeping track of time. One simply adds up the generations. Perhaps not the most accurate system, but I found it useful. And that was when I began studying California's history."

Nathan stared at the map in the dim light, trying to make sense of it. He could make out what appeared to be a coastline, but so many notations complicated it. Milton had scribbled in what seemed to be compass readings, place names, historical route lines and dates, and other indistinguishable markings. The old timer seemed to understand his own map intimately, and that was the important thing.

"As far as I can tell," Milton continued "the only known explorers in this part of the world close to that period of time were Cabrillo in 1542, Drake in 1579, Gali in 1584, Cermeno in 1595, and Vizcaino in 1602 and 1603. Of these, it appears that only Cabrillo and Vizcaino made it that far north. That was what I learned from the history books."

"You are convinced then that it was one of the Spanish explorers that cached this treasure?" Nathan asked.

"I am now. It is important to understand that the Spanish were interested in colonizing the pacific region. Both Cabrillo and Vizcaino were searching for suitable future Spanish ports for their trade routes, and to establish colonies. Sebastian Vizcaino believed he'd found a good harbor at Monte Rey, but continued to sail north in search of another.

"Officially, he carried no significant amount of wealth on his voyage. He sailed with four vessels; the *San Diego, Santo Tomas, Tres Reyes,* and a long boat. I could find no official records describing treasures on board any of these vessels, and began to dismiss the Yuki story."

Milton paused and took a sip of rum, and then continued his story.

"Although it is a matter of record that Vizcaino sailed north as far as the cape, and he made maps of the northern coast, the general belief is that none of his ships landed that far north. He reportedly turned back for home on January 19, Sixteen Hundred and Three.

"I was prepared to give up on the story altogether when I received a letter from a gentleman in Mexico City who claimed to be the descendant of one of the crew members of the *San Diego*. He had returned home from the voyage with the small number of survivors who hadn't perished due to scurvy, as so many of them did. In his letter this man claimed to have in his possession the original personal journal of his relative, and in the journal the writer described landing and caching two large chests in secret in the last part of the voyage. The purpose of the cache was explained to provide resources for a future colony, which had been the main objective of the expedition.

"Of course, all members of the voyage were sworn to secrecy, and the government of Spain, owing to a variety of circumstances including political changes and heavy losses in the Caribbean and the Atlantic, never followed through with the plans for colonization and control of Northern California north of Sonoma. There is good reason to believe they never returned to recover those chests.

"Naturally I was skeptical about the authenticity of this reported journal. This Mexican fellow learned of my interest in the voyage, he claimed, from a friend of his who'd seen my inquiries. So I traveled to Mexico City on his invitation, and for a fee he allowed me to transcribe sections of the document. I had a sense that he would have sold the original to me if I had offered sufficient payment. But it wasn't the document itself I was interested in, just its content. So I transcribed what I needed.

"It appeared genuinely old to me, and when I later translated what I'd copied into English, I encountered certain Spanish words and grammar not common to Nineteenth Century Mexican Spanish, but more fitting to an earlier period. I studied the language for more than a year during my analysis. And the writer described caching two chests in the rocks with an anchor forced into the hole to support the weight of a huge rock over the chests. That closely agrees with the Yuki story. I now believe that journal to be genuine."

"Will the Spaniards attempt to assert the treasure is their rightful property?"

"Currently nobody seems to acknowledge the existence of those chests, besides a few Indians. And the treasure was left in what is now our own country. Spain had several centuries in which to reclaim it, but wars and revolution seem to preoccupy her government lately. I believe it's anybody's treasure to claim. But I'm under no illusion that it will be easy pickings. We'll have to earn it, all right."

Milton poured the rest of the rum into Nathan's cup and anticipated his next question.

"But of course you wonder why this Mexican fellow or a relative before him hasn't come to claim the treasure."

Nathan nodded "Yes, that's …."

"The answer, I believe, is that we don't know for certain that he hasn't. However, the Yuki do not make any mention of it. And we should consider that the journal fails to identify the specific contents of those chests. It describes their purpose, but not precisely what is in them. Only a few men on the ship presumably had that information, and they apparently did not share it with the crew.

"Hence, we cannot be confident there exists any treasure at all. We can only hope it's there, and I suspect that it is, but cannot be sure. Those chests may merely contain carpenters' tools, or iron trade points for bartering with the natives, or even books for all we can speculate. But I've been to the cape, and I found what I believe to be the hole sealed with a bolder. I don't believe anyone's disturbed the cache in over two hundred years."

Nathan raised his cup to his lips and took a sip of the sweet tasting rum, and then spoke.

"Well, I understand we cannot predict just what we might find, but my own curiosity will not permit me to abandon the effort necessary to find out, so I'll be with you all the way on this endeavor."

"I was thinking you would feel that way, and I am mighty glad that you do." He raised his cup for a toast, and Nathan enthusiastically raised his to meet it. "To our hunt for the Spanish treasure!"

"The Spanish treasure!" Nathan echoed.

The next morning Milton woke up to the crackling of a revived fire in his fireplace, and in the confusion of flickering light perceived Nathan's silhouette stirring about at the hearth.

"Mighty eager to get started you seem to be, young man." He grumbled, sitting up and rubbing his one good sleepy eye. "What hour do you suppose it is?"

"Must be somewhere between midnight and maybe three or four," Nathan responded "but I no longer have a timepiece, so I can't be sure. I peeked outside the door, and it's still dark. Thought I'd heat up some coffee before we hit the trail. A few hot coals were still glowing from last night, and I decided to make use of 'em."

"Well, it's just as well. Sooner we get going, the better. It's a good stretch to Placerville."

A little more than a half-hour later, they left the cave and started down the mountain. Nathan was still barefoot, but his feet had already begun to toughen up, and he was no longer walking with a limp. He had every confidence now that he could make a trip like this, and he was certainly excited about it.

Nathan realized he was embarking on a truly extraordinary treasure hunt this time around, really unlike anything he had ever imagined. The old timer had investigated the related details for years, and was convinced he was on the right track. And even if he was wrong, the mere possibility of it being true was almost overwhelming. This was an exciting prospect indeed. And there was a mutual trust between them.

They didn't carry much with them besides canteens full of water, and of course their gold. Milton carried his Dragoon pistol in his belt, prepared for any trouble they might encounter. And they both agreed that a new sidearm for Nathan should be high on the list of priorities, and something to purchase before moving on to Sacramento.

The gold was divided into a series of separate pouches and carried equally between them. That way, if anything happened to one of them, they wouldn't risk losing all of it in one lump. Also, venders wouldn't be able to determine the amount they carried, and that would hopefully keep them honest with their prices.

They acquired their animals in Placerville and went on to Sacramento where hot baths, hot meals, and haircuts gave them a fresh start before heading off to the northern coast. Nathan bought his boots, long coat, and a factory-new Colt forty-four Model 1860 percussion Army revolver with a six-shot cylinder, a hundred caps, bullet mold, one-pound can of gunpowder, fifty lead balls, a grease tin, and a wooden cleaning rod to scrub out the barrel, all in Placerville, along with a new cowhide belt and a California slim holster for the Army revolver. He carefully loaded the weapon and test fired it several times at their first campsite after leaving Placerville. He was pleased with how it shot. It was a comfort to have a sidearm once again.

"What'll you do with your share of the treasure, should our best hopes be fulfilled?" Milton asked him.

Nathan sat close to the campfire, meticulously cleaning his new gun. He paused to consider the question.

"Well," he said "I met a fine young lady on my way to the Sierras, and I reckon I'll get us a place, and settle down some, just her and me."

Milton nodded with understanding. "Maybe you'd want to stop by and see her before we push on to the cape."

Nathan didn't say anything for awhile. He just continued wiping his revolver with a strip of cloth, thinking, occasionally adding sticks to the fire.

"No." He finally said. "No, I don't want her to see me in these rags, and looking like I do right now. When I go back to see her I'm going to look like a man of means. I'm going to have something worthwhile for her, before I go back."

"Let us hope so." Milton remarked. "But sometimes life isn't that simple. Some things bring us greater rewards than all the wealth in the world's hidden treasures."

CHAPTER VII

The late morning sun baked the sod grass and the trees across the landscape of the ranch, gradually warming everything before the full midday heat rose to its peak temperature during the summer months.

Emily had awakened earlier with a feeling of nausea she was not accustomed to, but managed to get herself up and out of the house before Mrs. Rhodes could notice. She had not felt like her usual spirited self lately. Instead, she found herself spending more time by herself, wherever she could escape the distraction of dialogue. And strangely, although she felt the desire to avoid everyone lately, she never felt so lonely in all her life.

It had been a month since Nathan had visited. It was time for him to return, as far as she was concerned, but she somehow knew that he wouldn't return for awhile. And she resented having to interact with anyone else. Even her own father, as much as she adored him, couldn't provide the kind of electricity she had experienced while Nathan was around. She had waited patiently and faithfully for a whole month, hoping he'd return to her by now, but he had not returned. Only a summer breeze crept up the winding dirt road, bringing swirls of dust and undefeatable quiet loneliness, but no glimpse of the man who stole her heart from her.

She began to cry. She hadn't cried in a long time until now. She could not even remember when she cried last, perhaps it wasn't so awfully long ago, but she never cried very often. She was, by her usual nature, too enthusiastic to cry over things. But she felt different this morning. She felt like crying.

Her mind was entertaining thoughts she didn't want to think about. Her body had been changing quite a lot over the last two years, but never had she experienced the kinds of things she'd been experiencing for several days, and she was terrified by what it all might mean. She wanted to talk about it with someone who knew a lot, someone like Mrs. Rhodes, but what would she think about Emily getting herself into such a fix? Nothing good could come from telling her, she convinced herself, even though she knew eventually it would be obvious when her belly started growing. That would be months away, hopefully. But she needed to talk to someone about it. She would think about telling Ann about it later that evening, maybe.

She decided to take her Scottish pony, Sunshine, out for a ride up the trail and maybe forget about all of it for awhile. It was too much for her to think about right now, she told herself. Her pony wouldn't entertain any such thoughts, and she envied the creature for its ignorance. Her own mind was cluttered with way too many troubles.

The heat of the sun bore down on her the way it had hundreds of times before, causing her to relish every brush of the wind, while she rode the same trail she'd been on at least as many times. The familiarity of everything around her helped her relax a bit, though her mood was different than usual. As hard as she tried, she could not get Nathan out of her mind.

James Ballou

The thought of how Mr. Thibault would feel about his daughter having a child out of wedlock was haunting her relentlessly, and she couldn't seem to escape it. She had no doubt that he wanted grandchildren, but not this way. She was filled with the greatest dread of her life over this situation, and there was no comfortable way out of it.

She spent most of the rest of the day in the company of Sunshine, riding to her favorite corners of the ranch and then resting under the shade of trees for a spell of tranquility while her friend grazed happily close by.

She'd been frequenting these secluded locations for as long as she could remember, and even before she had a pony to carry her to them. And she could find a temporary escape in them from life's more unpleasant matters, if only for a short time. After the death of her mother she sought the sanctuary of the forested patches beyond the eastside rolling hills, where she could gather her thoughts and contemplate life. And she found those moments beneficial to her soul.

Growing up, her father had been a helpful confidante in matters that troubled her, possessing wisdom and a kind of supportive nature she'd grown to cherish. But these current circumstances were unique, and presented a truly awkward element in her relationship with her father. This wasn't a problem she could easily approach him with. He had always been an understanding man, but how would he be able to understand something like this? She had a sense that she might have to face this thing alone, and that was an overwhelming thought. Even Nate, who was certainly a major component of her present dilemma, was not there to help her with it.

This day she had an awful lot to think on, and she spent most of it away from the house and alone. Alone except for the company of her pony.

Nathan previously had only read and heard about the vast magnificence of the ocean, but before this moment had

110

never seen any body of water so large that he couldn't see the other side.

The salty smell now reached his nostrils, carried up over the rocks by an ambitious sea breeze, and the Mendocino Lighthouse appeared to project itself majestically into view. Milton explained that the tower had been erected roughly two years earlier.

Nathan led the pack horses following Milton's lead to the rocks that he now began to actually recognize from the old timer's sketch on his map. His excitement was building as they approached the site Milton had marked on his map, and he noticed that it was shielded from the view of the lighthouse by large rocks. It appeared they should be able to work undetected, and he considered how fortunate that was.

They found what they hoped was the cache site just the way Milton had described it. There was a sizeable rock wedged into the mouth of an apparent hole slanting downward into the granite. It wasn't situated in an obvious location, and it didn't appear that it would be easy to find for anyone not specifically looking for it, and having some idea about what it might be.

"Those Spanish were clever all right," Nathan remarked "if this is what we hope it is."

Milton gave an agreeing nod "It wasn't exactly easy to find. I'd been up and down these rocks more than a few times before I stumbled onto this spot, quite by accident I might add."

They had acquired an impressive assortment of tools in Sacramento and considered themselves well equipped, but both of them were thinking the same thing. It was going to be a bear trying to remove that rock.

"Wonder how they figured Spanish settlers would ever uncork this bottle?"

"Same way we're going to, most likely."

James Ballou

Nathan decided to quietly observe Milton's actions initially, curious to see what he had in mind. At the same time, he contemplated possible strategies of his own, should their first efforts fail to move the stone. As difficult as the task appeared, however, Nathan was no longer inclined to underestimate Milton's practical senses. And after all, the old timer had survived quite well alone in a wild land by his own wits, and he'd had a long while to consider this task before them. His ideas were probably as practical as any.

"We've got no shortage of timberland." He said, scanning the countryside. "Our biggest concern might be conducting our operation without drawing attention to it. That lighthouse can't be more than a few hundred yards away, and our position is completely exposed to the open sea, and to every vessel that sails within observable range."

"Plenty lumber nearby to construct a sturdy framework." Milton said, gazing toward the trees and then back at the rock. "If we suspend those pulleys from a structure of stout timbers, we'll have a strong lift. And we'll need it. So we'll have to build it sound."

Among their gear was some tent canvas, and they both agreed that a tent would be the best way to hide the apparatus from anyone who might be passing by.

They didn't waste much time getting to work. Once Milton explained what he had in mind and Nathan was able to envision it, the tent went up. Trees were felled. Logs were cut, trimmed, dragged to the rock, and notched for fit.

It was an awkward location for such a structure. There wasn't much room for it. But they knew that if they had the right location, some sort of apparatus would most likely have been used by the Spaniards to lower the chests into the hole. The rock capping the entrance may have simply been dragged or rolled into position, if enough heavy ropes and horses were used to move it. It would be a challenge to pluck it out of the way, but the Spaniards must have had some kind of plan in mind for that. The whole trick might be to figure out what they had planned.

Several trees of six to eight inches in diameter, and a few slightly larger, were cut for the lift apparatus. The poles used for the tent were longer but smaller around. The two biggest of their four horses were employed in dragging the heavier sticks of lumber to the site. The woods weren't very far away, and that was much appreciated.

All of their activity, the chopping and working, made noise, and they wondered how long they might go before someone from the lighthouse would come around to investigate. The tower couldn't have been more than three or four hundred yards away at the most, and although the site was conveniently positioned in a blind spot outside direct view of the tower and the ocean waves created their own masking noises, the harvesting of trees from the surrounding forest was sure to draw attention.

Just as they expected, in the middle of the second day a man came around asking questions.

"Hello there!" He yelled.

Nathan, who had been boring a hole with a brace and auger bit through a short log he'd cut for a cross piece, looked up as the man walked down the path they'd been using to drag lumber.

"Name's Frank." The man explained, as he approached. "I'm the chief overseer of the Mendocino Lighthouse. Noticed a bit of activity down here and started gettin' curious. So, what is it you boys are up to, anyway?"

Nathan stood up and extended his right hand for a handshake. His feeling was that a polite gesture was the best way to greet their neighbor. The visitor instinctively shook his hand while Nathan introduced himself.

"I'm Nathan. And this…" He turned and nodded in the direction of the old timer, who had emerged from the tent upon hearing a stranger's voice. "This is Milton."

"How do you do?" Milton said, donning his brimmed hat to shade his face.

"Fine, thanks. Like I was just saying to your partner here, I'm in charge of the lighthouse. Came down to see what sort of operation you got going on here."

Nathan picked up the drill brace slowly, trying to think of a way to explain their activities.

"Exploration project." Milton blurted out. "We're here to investigate what's in these rocks."

"Geologists, then." The man who called himself Frank surmised.

"Well, technically no." Milton then added "But I'd say that's as close an explanation as I'd venture to endorse."

"Never figgered out much what compels scientists. But what you two do is right fine by me, so long's it don't bring no harm to the lighthouse, which I'm obliged to protect."

"You can rest assured your lighthouse is outside the scope of our interest, and we don't expect to camp here more than a couple days." Nathan declared, hoping to ease the man's concerns.

After the man walked away, Nathan began to resume his drilling through the log. Milton stood silently staring at the path the man left on, clearly distracted from his own task. Nathan noticed the old timer's unusual trance out of the corner of his eye, and stopped turning the brace.

"Kind of sorry I had to be misleading." Milton said. "Seems like a friendly enough young man. Dishonesty was never one of my characteristic traits, but what options were there?"

Nathan didn't comment, but instead nodded to convey that he understood.

"Of course," Milton continued "not a single word I spoke was untrue."

Nathan still offered no opinion, himself entertaining mixed thoughts.

"Even so, the deception cannot be denied." Milton finally admitted with a certain tone of acceptance. "I've got him convinced we're here for a scientific study."

"Do you predict he'll be back?" Nathan asked.

"Hard to say. But he didn't seem as curious about our enterprise as he was worried about his tower. I'd wager we're in the clear, at least for awhile. Had our treasure hunt taken us much closer to that building I believe we'd have encountered troubles with him."

Nathan resumed his drilling. "They hired on a loyal custodian when they employed that man." He remarked.

The treasure hunters got right back to work, assembling the apparatus they intended to support tremendous weight. Timbers were notched and fitted together, and a framework was soon erected, braced up wherever the greatest stresses were predicted.

They worked aggressively through the second day, only taking a few short breaks to guzzle fresh water and assess their progress. Nathan was impressed with how well the old timer was getting along, considering his age and the physical work this project demanded of both of them.

By the time the sun had disappeared into the ocean, they had their horses hobble tied for the night and Nathan and Milton were relaxing around the open fire watching the flames lick the outside of a cast iron pot. They used the same ring of stones and built the fire in the same spot where they had it the night before.

They were both physically exhausted and hungry after a full day of labor, but they felt good about their progress. The apparatus was basically complete, and the next day could be spent primary on dealing with that rock. And they were anxious to start on that rock. It was the remaining obstacle between them and whatever mystery rested beneath it.

"Suppose you're both wonderin' why Cecil was here this afternoon." Mr. Thibault said as he scooped up a mess of fried potatoes onto his plate.

"I saw his horse tethered by the barn," Ann said "but I wasn't going to ask."

"I was out with Sunshine all day. I didn't know that Mr. Haskins came by." Emily explained. She had planned to broach the awkward subject of her own dilemma during supper, but couldn't find it within her to do it just yet. This didn't seem to her at all like the proper time and place, and she started to really worry about when she would be able to talk about it, and how she ever would.

"Well, I'll tell you all about it then." He took a bite of potatoes, and chewed and swallowed quickly so he could begin telling what he was so enthused about.

"Cecil's buying cattle, and not just a few head. He found out about a rancher some three hundred miles to the south who's selling off his herd to go into breeding horses instead."

Mrs. Rhodes held a bite of potatoes on her fork over her plate to ask the question before starting to eat. "He rode all the way over here just to inform you that he's buying cattle?"

"Well, not entirely. See, the man wants to sell his whole herd of almost six hundred head. Cecil only wants to buy half. He came by this afternoon to see if I'd be interested in the other half. The price is twenty-five dollars a head if the rancher sells anything less than the whole herd in one deal. But he'll go twenty a head if he can sell them all."

"Are you buying three hundred head of cattle then, Father?" Emily asked, stirring the food around on her plate with her fork, realizing that she wasn't particularly hungry at the moment.

"Stew thinks the idea has merit. And like Cecil pointed out, most of them ranches down to the south are on desert terrain. Around here we've got excellent grazing, and we don't have any problems with water. I reckon we could fatten them up and grow the size of the heard. It's an opportunity to make a decent profit."

"Can you afford six thousand dollars, Jacob?" Mrs. Rhodes asked.

"Well, I sure don't have six thousand right now. But I'll need a bit more than that, anyway, considering the logistics involved in driving the heard up here. Every man and boy in the Haskin family is planning to go. Stew and I will go along, if it all works out. Might have to hire another two or three men. And it won't be easy at all, managing that size of a herd through some of those lower mountains and scattered timberland. Sure do wish that Mr. Clayburn was here to help us out. He's good with livestock. Saw how he does with his mule. Princess, when did you say he's supposed to return?"

A sensitive nerve was just touched. Emily had hoped Nathan would have returned by now. He'd been away for more than a month now, and she didn't know where he was, or how he was getting along. Her worst fear that he might actually never return entered her head, as much as she tried to ignore the unthinkable. The subject of Nathan Clayburn was suddenly an overwhelming subject, and she could bear her misery with a controlled face no longer. She exploded into a burst of teary emotion and excused herself from the table, retreating to the lonely isolation of her room upstairs.

Jake didn't know what to say, and remained silent for a moment. He looked at Ann, and neither of them felt much like talking or eating suddenly. Finally he broke the awkward silence.

"Didn't realize she was quite so tore up over him still. He was only here for the one day and night."

"She's young, Jacob. A day to her is like a year. But she's getting to that age where… Well, it probably won't be too much longer until she meets the right gentleman, and then her life will change drastically. You might as well get used to it."

"Not sure how to get used to losing my little Princess. But I know everyone has to grow up and live a reg'ler kinda life. I know it. Reckon I'll go up and have a talk with her after I finish these potatoes, which are mighty tasty by the way." He continued eating.

"You still didn't answer my question about how you're ever going to be able to afford those cattle."

He swallowed his food. "I'm fixin' on riding into Sacramento first thing in the morning, and I'll talk to Sam at the bank. I'm confident he'll extend the credit. This is a good plan, Ann. I've never felt so sure about any deal in my life. There's a lot of money to be made in cattle, and I figure I ought to be making some of it."

The treasure hunters were unable to budge the big rock even an inch all day. And they were feeling progressively frustrated.

Their first plan involved boring two holes into the top near the middle. One of them would turn an auger bit while the other would strike the blunt end of the shaft with a sledge repeatedly, causing the hard granite under the bit to break up and then turning the tiny rock chips out of the deepening hole.

It was hard, slow going, and they traded positions about every thirty strikes with the hammer. The plan also entailed sinking two hard spikes into the rock, which was the purpose for the holes; to give the spikes tight spaces to be forced into. Their shanks were ribbed to help them resist being pulled loose, and they had large eye loops for tying ropes to.

The two heaviest horses were initially connected to the leading end of the ropes by harness, and the hope was that together they could muster enough pulling power to dislodge the stone.

But it wasn't going to happen that way, and it took most of a day and a series of attempts to figure that out. Before the plan was finally abandoned, all four horses were eventually employed in the effort, and all connecting ropes were doubled for strength, but the stone still refused to leave the hole.

"Damned thing sure is wedged in snug." Milton mumbled with exasperation finally. "We may never pull it free with this method, even if we had twenty horses. We'll have to come up with a better plan."

"If I had my mule here right now, I would bet money that he could tip the scales in our favor. He's a brute." Nathan claimed, almost bragging.

The old timer wiped the sweat off his forehead. "Well, I sure do wish you had him here then. Right now we don't seem to have too much going in our favor."

Suddenly the memory of his mule, and how it had been taken away from him by a couple of thieving scoundrels became magnified under the present atmosphere of frustration, and Nathan's mood started to sour like stale vinegar.

"I ever catch those sonsabitches who stole my mule, I'll make them pay. They attempted to kill me. I need to make them wish they did."

Milton uncorked a canteen and took a quick drink, then handed it to Nathan, hoping that a swallow of fresh water would help cool down his mood.

"You'd be justified no doubt." Milton offered. "But I know a little something about revenge, and I don't remember it tasting quite as sweet as they say."

Nathan took a quick drink and handed the canteen back. "But those men are nothing but bad, and they deserve what they deserve." He insisted. "I ought to practice up with that new forty-four and go hunt them down, if we ever get our work done here."

"Some practice with that shooter of yours sure won't hurt. Being proficient with weapons can be mighty important out here in California.

"About that hunting them down business, I believe that an ambitious intelligent young man like yourself has better things to do."

"What's better than justice?" Nathan asked.

"Justice." The old timer repeated the word, searching his mind for an appropriate definition. "Ah, yes, that illusive ideal that taunts one's sense of morality. You can spend your years searching in vain, my good friend, if you expect to find justice out here.

"And how will you recognize it when you find it?" He went on. "One man's justice is arguably another's injustice. Everyone has his own perspective about it, and you can bet your money on that. Some consider horse thieving a hanging offense. That's their vision of justice, and who could say they're wrong?

"If you believe you can satisfy your want for justice by hunting those men down, then go ahead and hunt them down if you can. No reasonable man would question your right. But you've got a lot to think about on that score."

"Are you saying I should let them get away with it?"

Milton shook his head. "Nobody gets away with anything in this life. Of course, that's hard to visualize until you get old like me, when you get closer to the end of the rope, so to speak. But the whole point is that it has nothing to do with them. They've made their choices. It's all about you making some important choices that will shape the course of your own life. Think of that young lady you met. Maybe you have a future with her. Maybe that's the life you're meant to have. And that would sure beat chasing outlaws across the countryside."

"Well, I haven't much been able to get her out of my mind lately. That's a fact." Nathan acknowledged. "Tell me, Milton, do you believe it's possible for a man to have real feelings for a lady after just meeting her for the first time, after spending only one day together?"

"There are plenty different kinds of feelings, and as far as I know they're all real. An attraction between a man and a woman has its share of different dynamics. This whole matter about feelings and romance has been studied since ancient times no doubt, but I have as yet not seen a simple report on it. Perhaps destiny has something to do with the feelings men and women have for one another. Perhaps someday we'll know the truth about it."

Milton took another drink and then planted the canteen between two rocks, and sat down for a rest. It was starting to get dark, and there was an unspoken sense that no more progress was to be realized until they had at least one night to clear their minds. Nathan took a seat nearby. He was interested in what the old timer had to say. This was someone he knew had experienced many different things over the course of a relatively long life. He had wisdom. That much was clear. Nathan could learn from him.

"I had a wife." Milton said. "It was a long time ago, but she was a good woman. She and the son she gave me were both murdered by outlaws."

"That's an awful tragedy." Nathan commented with complete sincerity.

"Yes, it was. But I still remember the feeling I got the first time I set my eyes on her. So I have to say yes, I do believe it's possible, what you asked. Yes, indeed. But it still takes a mighty long time to get to know somebody properly. The main thing I think is to not be wasting too much of that precious time."

Jacob Thibault left early in the morning to go see the banker in Sacramento. He told Mrs. Rhodes not to expect him to return for a couple of days. He wanted a full day available, and maybe even two full days if necessary, to accommodate the banker's busy schedule. And Sacramento was close to thirty miles away from the ranch. Jake and the banker had done business together for years, but this whole thing with the cattle was different. He knew he was going to have to make a pretty strong pitch, if he was going to secure a loan to buy cattle. Maybe out in Texas the banks were eager to back the beef industry, but in the Sierra Nevada, just about everything was considered risky.

By the time Emily came downstairs her father had already left the ranch. Mrs. Rhodes was in the kitchen area stirring something.

"Well, isn't this a surprise?" Mrs. Rhodes remarked at seeing Emily descend the stairs. "I can hardly remember the last time you got yourself up in time to watch the sunrise."

"I know it, Ann. You are right. But I haven't been feeling like I normally feel."

Mrs. Rhodes stopped stirring and looked at Emily with scrutiny. "You aren't coming down with something, are you? You need to tell me if you've been running a fever."

"No, it's nothing like that. I'm sure it's nothing like that."

"Well you worry me, child. Your father's on his way to Sacramento right now, and we can't have him finding you sickly when he returns. That would trouble him deeply. Let me fry up some bacon and an egg for you. I'm preparing some dough right now for that bread you like so much."

"I know. I can smell it. Can I help you, I mean, *may* I help you bake it?"

"That depends. Are you sure you're well enough?"

"Well enough to bake bread."

"All right, then. I'll need some eggs. And I added too much water to the mixture. A tiny bit more flour should be added to thicken it up. I already put that bag of flour away. If you could grab it out of the cupboard for me…"

"Ann, do you believe in love at first sight?"

Mrs. Rhodes resumed her stirring. "So that's it. I see now. You're lovesick. I guess I kind of had that impression last night at supper. Well I'm glad that's all it is. I don't believe there's ever been a young lady who hasn't come down with that sickness at least two or three times while growing up. But fortunately for you, it isn't usually terminal."

"That's because it's worse than terminal." Emily replied.

Mrs. Rhodes laughed. "I'm sorry, Emily, I really don't mean to laugh. You have such a way with words sometimes, though, and I can't help myself. But I know the misery that accompanies lovesickness. I remember my first episode, when I was close to the same age you are now, and I thought the world would come to an end.

"If it makes you feel any better, the sickness *does* go away. You'll get over it and move on with your life, eventually. Of course, that might seem impossible to you now. But you're young. Things are so much larger than life, when you're young.

"When you're older you'll have a better perspective, but you won't gain that without some pain. And that young man, Nathan Clayburn, will be merely one among others whose life will have briefly crossed the path with yours. But no matter how we try to avoid certain kinds of suffering, it's part of life. These things are hard but they help us grow."

"But what if I'm carrying his child?"

Mrs. Rhodes stopped stirring suddenly and stared at Emily, with a horrified look on her face. "What?!? Please tell me you're not suggesting… My dear girl, we must pray it isn't true."

James Ballou

"But I think it *is* true, Ann. I've had some strange symptoms. Lately I've felt like I've never felt before."

Mrs. Rhodes could not hide the look of panic in her eyes.

"Oh, dear. What are we going to do with you? That Mr. Clayburn was only here for one night. Are you sure it isn't something else that's causing you to feel the way you feel?"

"I'm not sure of anything anymore." Emily said with tears streaming down her cheeks. "I don't know what to do about it. I don't know what father will do when he finds out. How can I tell him?"

"Jacob is a reasonable man. But you better let me talk to him first. It might help for him to hear about it from someone with some years. This would be considered something of a scandal where I come from, but out here it might be different."

"What will it do to him?" Emily asked, desperately worried about hurting her father.

Mrs. Rhodes again resumed stirring nervously. "Well, as I said, your father is a reasonable man. He's always been an understanding man. This whole thing is partly my fault for not teaching you better how to manage yourself in situations of having to resist physical advances from men. I should have made sure you were prepared for this sort of thing. But I just didn't think you'd be crossing this bridge so soon."

"But *I* made the advances. Nate didn't make any advances. It was all my doing, Ann."

"Well, Mr. Clayburn certainly played a part in it, didn't he? And where is he now? When do you expect to see him again? That young man is not blameless in this, but he sure has left you with the problem. You shouldn't defend him."

"What will I do?"

"You will let me try to explain everything to Jacob when he returns."

CHAPTER VIII

After another three days of hard work, trying unsuccessfully to remove the rock blocking the hole suspected of hiding Spanish treasures, the task began to seem impossible, and really more like a waste of precious time. Not only were their food supplies fast being exhausted, but so were their ideas about methods of extraction. They'd tried every combination of ropes, horses, levers, blocks & tackles, and mechanical advantage they could devise to no avail. And Nathan was getting increasingly anxious to see Emily again.

As they sat around their campfire after another long unfruitful day, they talked about taking down the tent and the apparatus in the morning and leaving the dream of discovery behind, at least for now.

"If we had something to blow that rock out with," Nathan wishfully theorized "like a whole lot of gunpowder maybe, sure would've saved us a lot of headaches."

"Gunpowder likely wouldn't do it." Milton explained. "You would need a high explosive, such as nitroglycerine, or whatever they use these days. But if we blew that rock, we'd surely risk destroying whatever might rest beneath it. I thought of that idea already."

"I suppose you're right. Makes sense, anyway. But what do you think the chances are that any treasures are actually under there? I mean, would they have gone to such extremes to hide it?"

Milton shook his head. "I'm not as confident about it as I was when I first stumbled onto this site. I think people will go to any lengths to hide wealth, but it seems more and more unlikely to me that anyone would choose a spot like this, given its inconvenient location. If they did cache something here, it could conceivably only be because the cape is a perfect natural landmark for reference."

"We can always come back in the spring and take another crack at it." Nathan said, trying to sound optimistic in the face of defeat. Milton couldn't think of much else to say. He didn't feel much like talking.

It was a restless night for both of them. A lot had been invested in this endeavor, and the realization that it had all been for nothing was something neither was really prepared for. Their disappointment was huge, more than either could admit, and their plan to disassemble the apparatus the following day and pack up for the trip home made it especially difficult to think about anything else, or even to fall asleep anytime soon.

Before the sun was up high enough to light up the morning on the coast, Nathan was out from under his blanket and gathering up tools, at least those he could see in the gray of dawn. The sooner they could be packed up and out of the area, the better. The ocean was breathtaking in its natural grandeur, and he realized he would miss the salty breezes and scenic beauty, but this place was a symbol of disappointment to him now. It would be several years before he would really want to return, he thought to himself.

He could hear Milton snoring, still rolled up in his blanket on the ground over by the now cold smoldering fire pit. Nathan planned to have a pretty good start on dismantling the apparatus before the old timer woke up.

He decided to take down the big tent first, starting with untying the ropes it was suspended by, after setting down his armload of tools, but that bolder distracted him. There it was, stubbornly unmovable from where it had remained the focus of their attention for days, and it seemed to taunt him now, as if it were secretly laughing at their failure to move it.

Nathan reached for a pickax from the pile of tools and gripped the handle firmly with both hands. He expected the hard granite to blunt the pick's point, and the force of the hard swing to possibly break the wooden handle, but he didn't care. It would be his final act of defiance against the stubborn rock. He would vent his built up frustration and disgust of the obstacle before continuing to clear the site.

The pickax was raised high over his head and then brought down swiftly onto the rock with all the force he could apply, and he closed his eyes as he delivered the blow, anticipating flying rock chips and the head of the ax bouncing off the rock in an unpredictable direction.

But to his surprise the tool didn't bounce off the rock. Instead, the point of the pick embedded itself into the stone, wedged firmly into a crack the blow had caused. Nathan tried to remove the head, but it was stuck in the rock.

He examined the surface of the rock more closely in the available early morning light now entering the area where tent canvas had just been untied and folded back. There was a crack across the entire top surface of the rock, linking the several holes they had drilled for the spikes.

The rock was cracked. It appeared likely cracked completely through the mass of its body. And it was caused by a single blow of an ax!

This was an exciting situation. It meant that the impossible stone could be defeated after all. It could be broken up into smaller, manageable chunks that could be lifted out of the hole. It would require continued perseverance, still without any guarantees, but it was clearly an achievable objective. This situation changed everything, and Nathan could see that. He suddenly began to feel a renewed inspiration.

He woke Milton up immediately and explained the latest revelation. As soon as the groggy old man was awake enough to process the information, he rose to his feet and followed Nathan up the path to the big tent. This morning they didn't even bother to heat up coffee or eat any breakfast. They both wanted to get right to work. The goal was no longer moving, prying, or pulling the heavy stone out of the hole. Now they would work to reduce the mass into smaller pieces, and remove the smaller pieces from the mouth of the hole.

Efforts were now focused on boring a series of new holes into the rock and driving long spikes into those holes, forcing new cracks to form. They had log wedges among their tools for splitting trees, and these they hammered into the cracks to accelerate the breaking process. Much of this was the same kind of work they had accomplished over the previous days. The main difference this time was that now they were confident they would eventually reach their objective. These new holes drilled into the stone, obtained with a good deal of sweat and exertion just like the first holes they drilled, now had a proven purpose. Cracking the rock and breaking it up seemed like such an obvious approach to moving the obstruction as to cause Nathan and Milton to both wonder why neither had thought of it before.

When a web of new cracks began to appear in the rock, they knew that it wouldn't be long before they'd be able to hook onto one of the chunks and lift it out. The remaining pieces would then be much easier to remove one by one.

"Do you figure this is what the Spanish had in mind?" Nathan wondered.

"I don't think we'll ever know for certain." Milton responded. "We sure beat up a lot of tools trying all those other ideas I spent years planning out, though. But wouldn't it be something if after all this work we find out there's nothing to the story?" He started laughing at the thought.

"I reckon we'll know pretty soon." Nathan said, securing ropes to spikes embedded in the smallest chunk, and feeding them through the pulleys over their heads. He then took the running end down the path and dropped it ten feet away, where he could guide the horses. A few moments later he had ropes attached to harnesses, and with his guidance and the available horsepower, the first chunk of granite was lifted out of the mouth of the hole.

This was viewed as a major achievement, and the two men took a break and drank some water. The ocean breeze helped evaporate the sweat off their faces and cool them down somewhat. But Nathan noticed that Milton's face looked unusually pale, and the old timer didn't appear to be breathing very easy.

"Are you holding up all right? You don't look so well." Nathan expressed with concern.

"I believe I just need to rest here a spell, and catch my breath." He found the nearest flat rock to sit on for a moment.

"Well, I think we got the hardest part done." Nathan assured. "The rest is basically a one-man operation, as far as I can tell. The horses will do the real work from this point on, with just a little guidance from me."

After draining his canteen, Nathan proceeded to hook onto one chunk of bolder after another and compel the horses to lift them out of the hole. The excitement intensified with each new extraction until Milton could sit back and watch no longer. He joined Nathan at the edge of the hole where they strained to see down into the dark space.

"We're almost there." Nathan explained. "Just a few more chunks of granite between us and what we came here for." He looked at Milton. "How do you feel now?"

"Well I'm still breathing. I don't know what came over me there all of a sudden like, but it seems to have passed. Age has a way of putting limits on a man."

Less than a half hour later a rust covered iron ship's anchor became visible, and at that point there was no more doubt about the credibility of the story. This was indeed the cache the Indians were talking about, and it was hidden exactly the way it had been described.

Nathan climbed down into the hole that now existed, to determine how this big iron object might be dislodged, and to tie on the ropes. It was a good thing they built such a stout apparatus, he thought. It was going to take a lot of strength to hoist it up out of the hole.

While he was down in the hole, his boots found the top of a flat object to stand on, and although he couldn't see what it looked like without a candle or lantern, he knew exactly what it was. There would be plenty of time to examine the cache later. Right now his focus was on lifting everything out of the dark hole in the rock. Milton offered to lower a lantern down into the hole, but it wasn't needed to tie the ropes where he wanted them tied. Besides, there wasn't much room to work in that hole. He didn't want to mess with a lantern in such tight confines.

When the first of the two chests was hoisted out of the mouth of the hole, suspended by ropes, its actual state of deterioration became visible to examining eyes for the first time in more than two and a half centuries. The hardwood boards comprising most of the box, though partially rotted away and badly weathered, were held intact for the most part by severely rusted thick iron straps. It wasn't a particularly huge crate, as their imaginations envisioned, but a more modest trunk roughly the size of a clothing basket.

But the apparent strain on the ropes suggested a substantial amount of weight within. The lid was latched and locked closed with a large heavily corroded iron padlock.

Once they had it lowered onto the rocky ground, they were able to ponder over how they should open it.

"That's a mighty big lock on that latch." Milton commented, itching to find out what the box contained. "Wonder where they hid the key?"

Nathan drew his revolver from its holster and thumbed back the hammer. "Maybe a couple blasts from a forty-four will persuade it to open up."

Milton raised his hand to discourage any discharge of a firearm under the current circumstances.

"It isn't likely that a lead ball out of a revolver would make much of an impact on a thick chunk of iron. Besides, the noise would surely get that Frank's attention. He'd likely come around asking questions." Milton suggested. "One of our pry bars would be the tool to use here. Slip it through the lock and twist the thing open."

The lock broke open without too much effort, by using one of the long pry bars. Opening the lid required some prying with the bar as well, because the hinges were very nearly rusted solid.

At first there didn't appear to be anything in the chest besides plenty of rotted wood dust and scraps of decaying material resembling leather-bound documents. It wasn't until Nathan began scooping out the badly deteriorated debris from within the box that his fingers found the unmistakable cold metallic disks that seemed to fill the bottom half of the chest. He lifted his fist out of the chest and opened his hand under the close inspection of Milton's one good eye.

"God Almighty, Nathan, we've struck pay dirt! It's a Spanish treasure after all. You've got five, no, six pieces in your hand there. They look Spanish, and they look old."

Nathan looked at the coins and inspected them closely himself. They were silver pieces of varying sizes, partially tarnished, and obviously Spanish.

"The whole bottom half is full of them." He said.

The second chest was lifted from the hole in the same manner as the first, by tying the ropes to the iron rings mounted at each corner of the box lid. It proved to be a more difficult task with the second chest, because it rested at the bottom of the hole in a tighter, darker working space.

In order to be able to reach the second chest with his hands whereby he could secure it by ropes, Nathan descended into the hole head first, being suspended by an extra rope tied around his ankles and controlled by Milton using the system of pulleys to manage Nathan's body weight. Nathan had to work upside down and judge his knots by feel, because it was simply too dark to be able to see very much at all down there, and a lantern would be awkward to manage in that position.

Milton struggled hoisting Nathan back up after he had the ropes tied to the chest and signaled to be brought back up. By now the physical exertion was taking its toll on him.

The second chest contained more impressive valuables than the first. While the first chest housed mostly old silver coins and glass trade beads, the second was loaded with gold pieces and decoratively embellished items such as crosses and daggers.

Nathan scooped up one handful after another of gold and silver coins and miscellaneous other jewels and decorative pieces, and heaped them into a growing pile on the ground for closer inspection. Milton removed his trusty magnifying lens from its leather pouch, and studied the array of treasures before him, piece by piece. Sorting through all of it was obviously going to take some time, and they both finally decided to take down the tent and apparatus and pack up for home, where they could study their newly acquired wealth in a more secure environment.

When Milton stood up on his feet he nearly toppled over, grabbing the frame of the apparatus for support. His magnifying lens fell from his shaking fingers and almost rolled into the hole where the chests had been. Nathan saw it rolling on its edge and swept it up before it could fall into the hole. He noticed that it was chipped on one edge from the drop. He tried to hand it over to Milton, but the old timer was struggling to hold onto the framework, to keep from falling over.

Nathan grabbed him by the arm and helped him sit down safely. He knew right then that his friend was in trouble. It was probably the exhausting work of the recent days putting a dangerous strain on him, or simply being overwhelmed by the enormity of this almost unbelievable treasure, or possibly even a combination of both. But whatever the cause, he was clearly not well.

"We need to get you to a doctor." Nathan said. "Does your map show where the nearest town is?"

Milton shook his head. "No doctor is capable of stopping the effects of old age."

"You're not well. I have to help you get well. I owe a debt, remember? You saved my life, and now I've got the responsibility of…"

Milton interrupted. "I'm near my end, young man." By now his hand was trembling violently. "Nothing you or any doctor can do will change that. This way I'm feeling I've never felt before, and I know what it means."

Nathan had no immediate comment. Before this day he had not seen Milton as anything besides strong and fit. Indeed, he'd been stronger and fitter than he looked. But he looked anything but fit now, and this certainly wasn't anything at all expected.

"Well there must be something I can do for you." Nathan said.

"My time is close, Nathan, and nobody can do anything to change that." The words came out with some difficulty, and he was breathing harder now. "But you can help me. You can take me back to my home up in those mountains, and after I leave this world, bury me there. That's what you can do for me. I don't have any living relatives that I'm aware of. I belong to the mountains. I should be with the hawks, the bears, and the deer."

"As you wish." Nathan consented out of respect for his friend.

"We'll split the treasure evenly, just like we agreed," Milton continued "but since I won't be around to enjoy my half, I have a small request to make of you concerning that."

"Just name it." Nathan said.

"I want you to find a charitable use for it. I want you to find somebody who's run on hard times, and help that individual."

"I will set your part aside for only that purpose, and search for someone in need." Nathan agreed.

"Very good then." Milton leaned his head back against the rocks. His eyelid looked heavy. "Do that, and you will have paid back your debt."

Nathan wasn't sure how close the old timer was to his end, but he suspected a lot closer than he'd expected. Milton was beginning to relax a bit, lying on the rocky ground, his uncovered eye now closed, and his breathing more regular now.

"How much time do you think you've got left?" Nathan asked.

There was a lapse of nearly a full minute before Milton responded to his question, during which time Nathan wasn't sure whether or not his friend had fallen into his long sleep already. Then suddenly he spoke.

"I don't know. Not long. But if you're able to take down the structure and pack us up proper before we start back, it will be best. You don't want to leave clues behind for marauders. I apologize that I won't be much help to you now."

"No need to worry about that." Nathan assured him. "I'll have it all down in short order. We'll leave hardly a trace."

The realization that Milton wasn't going to be around much longer caused Nathan to start thinking a lot about what that meant. It meant he would be saying good-by to an important friend. He'd be saying good-by to someone who had saved him, and helped him get back on his feet after he'd been knocked all the way down. His mind remained occupied with these things while he went about dismantling the apparatus.

"How did you know you could trust me when you found me out there in a state of such disaster?" Nathan asked while the opportunity to do so still existed.

"I didn't." Milton responded, struggling now even to speak. "Sometimes you have to take a chance on people, I suppose. Was never too good at that myself, but I was fulfilling an obligation.

"Of course, when you came to, I sensed something genuine about you. You didn't hide your reason for roaming alone in the Sierra Nevada. I didn't figure you were too smart, but you were honest. I've come to change my mind about your intelligence, but I know I was right about your honesty. It's an honorable trait."

"I came to California to find gold, all right. But prospecting isn't always seen as such an honorable pursuit."

"That may be true in some circles, but it sure brought a lot of folks out to this part of the world. Most were prospectors, or at least made their way because of prospectors. I've been a prospector now for a good portion of my years." He experienced a short coughing spell before resuming the discourse.

"You're a fine man, Nathan, and I mean it. But I want you to remember what I told you about that matter of revenge. It never did anyone a bit of good. Those men who tried to kill you failed, so you've already got your revenge in that. Now it's time to let go of that part of your life. You've got better things to look ahead to."

Nathan thought about his words, and continued working while he thought about them. Milton appeared to have more to say, but it was clearly a struggle for him. After a few minutes he started talking again, and Nathan took a break from the work to listen.

"I want you to have my guns and books and other effects. I don't have anyone else to leave them to, so I'm leaving them to you."

"Thanks."

"Nathan?"

"Yes. I'm right here."

"Nathan, I'd have been proud if you'd been my son."

Nathan set the sledge down and looked at Milton, who was lying on his back with a look on his face that revealed his suffering, though he remained calm.

"Well I'd have been proud to be your son. Won't ever forget you, you know."

Nathan folded a blanket and placed it under Milton's head to help him rest more comfortably, and then let him alone so he could get some sleep while he continued tearing down everything they'd built. He used some of the lumber to fill in the hole in the rock, and then he collected up some rocks, dirt, branches and leaves and covered over the top of the hole. The remaining timbers were hauled a short distance away and hidden under some thick brush.

Before sundown he had the horses all packed and nearly ready to travel. When Milton woke up he was surprised to see how well the site had been restored to natural.

"What did you do with the treasure?" He asked, his eye searching for the two chests.

"I emptied those chests and filled the canvas bags we bought. It's all packed on the horses. The chests didn't appear salvageable, so I buried them back in the hole where we found them, along with some of the boards from the apparatus."

"That's right smart thinking. Actually had the same idea myself. Looks like we're ready to depart then, if I can get myself up."

"I'll help you up onto your horse, if you feel up to traveling." Nathan looked toward the west where the sun appeared to dip into the ocean. "It'll be dark soon, but we don't have to travel tonight if you'd prefer to rest some more."

"I've been resting all afternoon. I'm in favor of not waiting."

"Good enough." Nathan brought Milton's horse up the pathway and assisted him into the saddle with some difficulty. The old timer was in bad shape now, and Nathan realized things would only get worse for him from this point forward. Though he was anxious to see his home and his garden before he left this world, he was clearly in for a miserable journey, and he knew it. But his need to return home was a powerful one. Powerful enough to endure the saddle for several days straight while feeling worse than he had ever felt before.

Mrs. Rhodes woke Emily up at seven o'clock in the morning. That was considered late for anyone in the country with chores to tend. It was also later than Emily had ever been used to sleeping. But a number of things in her life had been quite different lately.

"They've left already, your father and Stewart with those cowpunchers your father hired, and the Haskins bunch. They all rode out of here over an hour ago, after finishing the pancakes I served them." Mrs. Rhodes said. "Now it's up to just the two of us to look after the ranch for the next couple weeks. We've got plenty of chores. I've got my work in the kitchen, and you've got animals to tend. The sooner you get yourself up, the better."

"Ann, did you have that talk with Father before he left?"

"As a matter of fact I did."

"Well?"

"Well he didn't have much to say, except that he would do a lot of thinking about it on the cattle drive. I thought I explained your situation as well as it could be explained, and he listened. It's probably a fitting time for him to be getting away for awhile. He's got plenty now to think about, and as quiet as he was after I told him, I'm certain his mind was doing a lot of thinking already."

"Ann?"

"Yes? What?"

"Thanks. I can't imagine how I could ever survive without you."

Mrs. Rhodes turned to exit Emily's bedroom. "Someday you will, you'll see. But time's getting on, young lady, and we've both got chores to tend."

After what was for Milton some grueling days of travel, the prospectors arrived back in the mountains where the comforts of the cave awaited them. And it was none too soon, as either of them was concerned, because the first hints of autumn were in the chilled breezes sweeping down from the north, and the sunny days were getting shorter.

"It's a hard winter that's coming." Milton said with a quivering voice as they sat hunched over their last campfire the night before reaching the cave. "Was a hotter than usual summer in the valley, which probably means it'll be a colder than usual winter in the mountains. But I don't expect to be around to see the end of it."

"Well I hope you're wrong about that – about you not livin' much longer. I didn't figure I'd make it after those scoundrels got hold of me, but I'm still here. Maybe it's the same with you. Maybe you'll lick this illness that's pinching your strength."

"This illness is called old age, my friend, and it's more than I can lick. But I've had my share of years, and some of them were plenty good. We all have our time."

Nathan opened his hands palms down over the flames to warm them. "You'd know more about that than I would, I reckon." He said.

A cool wind suddenly stirred the embers of the fire, and chilled Nathan even in his wool vest.

"I've lost track of the days." He said. "I would guess this is August, but with all that's happened since I first arrived in California, I stopped counting days. It was mid-June when I boarded the train out of Nebraska, so I'm guessing this is August. But it seems awfully cold for August, at least where I'm from."

Milton's eye peered up into the night sky as if to read the time of year by the stars. "I'd say we're into September already." He said. "Never felt the fall of the year in August like I feel it now. Must be September."

"Well, maybe so. But September's still a stretch away from winter."

The old timer's ailing face forced a smile at the comment.

"September nights can feel like winter in the mountains. But you'll have to experience that for yourself to know what I'm talking about. And then, before you know it, these mountains will be buried under a thick silky blanket of snow. Nothing prettier I've ever seen. You'll see what I mean plenty soon enough."

When they finally reached the cave, Nathan helped Milton down off his horse and then unpacked the tools, treasure bags, and the rest of their supplies.

"Won't have much use now for the two pack animals." Nathan said. "I can take them down to Placerville tomorrow and sell them back to that fella we bought 'em from. We should recoup at least some of our investment."

"Sell my riding horse with the others." Milton requested. "I won't be needing him again, now that I'm home. I'm done with riding."

"As you wish. I'll leave at first light. I'll make us a fire in awhile and heat up some of whatever we got left to eat. I'll be getting some food staples in town when I get there."

"We could sure use some corn flour. I might still have some carrots in the ground. You can check in the morning. Might even have some potatoes left, but a lot of what I planted fed other critters, so you may not do so well with those. If you don't find any in the garden, you might purchase about ten pounds, if it's not too much trouble to haul them back. I sure got a hankering for fried potatoes."

"I should also bring back some fresh meat. I'll buy some cuts of beef if available. If not, then I'll do some deer hunting after I get back. But I think you need that in your diet to help you get your strength back." Nathan said.

Milton sat leaning back against a tree just outside the front door of his cave as Nathan finished unloading their horses, and suddenly he began a coughing spell that tortured him until he could no longer sit up. Nathan dropped what he was doing and helped the old timer into the cave to his bunk. He lit the candle on the table and started toward the door to finish with the horses.

"I'll secure the animals for the night, and then I'll get us some soup put together and get that fire going. We can inspect and count our riches after a good meal if you're up to it. But I've got things under control out there, so you might as well try to rest up 'til I get back."

"Maybe that's the problem." Milton said. "I haven't done much else for days."

"Well you've needed some rest all right, and it doesn't look like you're done with needing it just yet."

"I'll have plenty of time for resting when I'm dead."

"Yeah, well maybe a little rest now won't do you any harm. You sure don't have to worry about it killing you. Besides, that resting in the saddle trick doesn't count for much. You've got a better situation here, and I know you'll agree with that."

Milton nodded but didn't speak, hoping to avoid another violent coughing spell. But he knew Nathan was right. Anything would be easier to endure than the trip home had been. He was glad to be home.

After consuming the last of their soup ingredients later that evening, Milton forced himself to sit up at the table where the two of them worked under a lantern, sorting through the Spanish riches for several hours. They worked steadily counting, categorizing, and making a record of what they had recovered. The sheer magnitude of the treasure made this an exhausting endeavor for Milton in his current state, but the excitement of it all kept him at the table.

Finally, when they were done counting all that they had recovered, they discovered they had over two-thousand Spanish silver Pieces of Eight, another three-hundred and twenty smaller silver coins, more than five-hundred gold pieces of which nearly four-hundred were close to an ounce each in weight. In addition to the coins, there were precious stones, beads, gold and silver crosses, and ornamental daggers. Much of it was beyond their ability to properly evaluate, but they both knew they possessed a substantial sum in value.

"I could never have imagined finding a treasure like this." Nathan confessed.

"I've had plenty of time to let my own imagination get the better of me on more than one occasion," said the old timer "but I would never have believed something like this if I hadn't seen it for myself, not in a hundred years."

The following morning Nathan left with the horses. He returned to the rancher from whom the animals were purchased only weeks before, and sold three of them back to him as intended, allowing the man a generous profit.

After he'd received his payment, something caught his attention out across the pasture. His eyes widened, and he focused his concentration. He was certain about what he saw, and he could hardly believe it. It was the same mule he'd bought in Sacramento. It was the same size and the same bay coloring.

"You look like ya might be inarest'd in that mule over there, mister. I can make you a right good deal on 'im, if y'are, though mules can fetch a hefty price in the high country."

"Where'd you get him?" Nathan asked flatly.

"Bought 'im from two fellars what came through town not more'n a week ago. He's a little jumpy, but he's seemed to settle down some since I've had 'im."

"Did you get their names, those two men?"

"They wrote me a bill o' sale, but I cain't read their signatures."

"Do you know where they are now?" Nathan expressed an intense interest.

The man took off his hat and scratched his head. "No, they didn't say where they was headed. Least not to me, they didn't. Say, what's this all about? Why're ya so durned curious about them, anyhow?"

"Because that mule belonged to me. I bought him in Sacramento from a rancher named Carl Lewiston. I was camped up in the hills when those two men jumped me and near killed me, then took my mule and other provisions and left me for dead."

The man became defensive. "Now hold on there, mister, I paid good money for that animal, but I had no reason to think I was getting' stolen property. Now, if you can show me a bill o' sale, well, I s'pose that'd be a different story."

Nathan shook his head. "Don't have it anymore. Look, what happened to me on account of those two men is between them and me. Just because I was robbed doesn't mean you should be, too. You paid good money for that mule, and there was no way you could've known he was stolen. I'm willing to pay you your fair price, just to get him back."

The tension between them suddenly faded. "Tell ya what, mister, mules can cost twice as much as a good horse in the Sierras. Now if you want to make an even trade, I'll accept your horse. I know he's a good horse, 'cause I sold 'im to ya. But I'll do ya that deal if you want it."

"That's plenty fair, sir, and you've got a deal." Nathan accepted without hesitation, glad to get his friendly mule back.

CHAPTER IX

By now Nathan was especially anxious to see Emily again, and he considered making a brief visit to the Thibault Ranch before returning to the cave. It wasn't a great distance from Placerville, and he guessed he could do it and it would only extend his trip by maybe two days altogether.

But the more he thought about it, the more he decided against it. That old timer wasn't up to looking after himself for the time being, and he would be struggling without the food he depended on Nathan to bring back. It would be a long wait for him as it was, and mighty cruel if Nathan didn't return directly. So Nathan purchased a good supply of basic food provisions and headed straight back to Milton's cave in the mountains. Once the old timer got back on his feet, Nathan decided, it would be time to go visit Emily again. Surely that wouldn't be too much more time. Good food and a lot of rest should put the old timer right. That seemed like a reasonable expectation. But there could be no leaving him alone very long before he'd recovered enough to take care of himself.

When Nathan returned to the cave he found Milton in a terrible state. He was unable even to get himself up from his bunk, and it was clearly an effort for him to eat anything at all. Nathan realized that if he had taken that detour he had contemplated taking, he would have likely found his friend dead by the time he returned. The old timer was in desperate need of a lot of help, and he appeared sicker than Nathan had yet seen him.

"Should've gotten you to a doctor when I had the chance, that's what I should have done."

Milton tried to respond but interrupted himself with a horrible coughing fit that almost turned into vomiting. And the patch that had covered his eye was now lying on the floor of the cave next to his bunk, exposing a hideous old scar. He was an awful mess, and his suffering was a hard thing for Nathan to watch. At that point there didn't appear to be much hope for him. But Nathan could remember when his own condition seemed hopeless, and it wasn't so awfully long ago, so he wasn't prepared to give up on the old timer.

"You should go see that young lady friend of yours before it's too late." Milton said, when he was finally capable of uttering a discernible phrase.

Nathan temporarily stopped stirring the stew in the pot over the fire, surprised to hear words from Milton. "I intend to, just as soon as we get you back up on your feet."

Milton tried to sit up, but lacked the strength. "Then you could be a long time waiting. I may never get back up again."

"Well, you'd die for certain without any help in your condition, and I can't have that on my conscience."

"The only thing worse than dying is not being allowed to when your time comes." The old man grumbled in his misery.

"I reckon only the Good Lord knows when your time should come," said Nathan "and I don't figure He'd be for me leaving you alone so helpless. No decent man would even consider leaving his sick friend to die, and I won't. You might as well get used to that."

The weather turned colder, and Milton's condition hadn't improved after more than a month at his cave. Nathan tried everything he could think of to help his friend recover; he kept a warm fire going night and day, collected plenty of fire wood, cooked healthy meals, and helped the old man up and about for regular exercise, and when he needed to go outside to relieve himself. He could never have managed those things on his own in his state.

As time went on, there seemed no end in sight to the situation. Some days, Milton was so ill it didn't look like he'd survive to see the next. Then, unexpectedly, he would appear to be improving very slightly, and Nathan would naturally get his hopes up. But the better moments never lasted long, and Milton's condition would soon deteriorate to a worse state than it had been previously.

"Oh why doesn't the Lord just take me now, and save us both endless agony?" He started asking aloud during his worst suffering, which had become a daily experience.

"I don't reckon life is meant to be easy." Was Nathan's response. "There are probably reasons for these things that we can't know right now. Maybe we're all being put to some kind of test."

"If that's true, I'd say you've already passed your test. Now it's time you moved on to your next lesson. Go on and see that young lady you told me all about. No need for you to stay here even another day. Go on, go see what life has for you."

"As long as you're sick and too weak to take care of yourself I'll go nowhere."

Milton realized he couldn't convince Nathan of what he thought he should do, in spite of the obvious hopelessness of his own condition, and he ran out of energy trying. Nathan was a determined young man, and there was no persuading him on matters about which he had a strong ethical conviction. It was what Milton had come to admire most about him in the relatively short time he'd known him, but it was sure a source of his frustration now. He even pondered putting his pistol to his own head and ending the burden for both of them, but his Colt Dragoon wasn't currently within his feeble reach, and he knew Nathan wouldn't be a party to such a plan. Without his help he couldn't get to the gun, which was hanging from a peg on the wall. Probably if his pain was visibly severe enough his friend would do him that favor, but he wouldn't be considered at that stage just yet. Nathan was still talking about hope and recovery. The old man knew it was all for nothing. It was nothing more than a prolonging of his suffering.

Jacob Thibault returned to the ranch with his newly acquired herd after an arduous journey across a wide range of diverse terrain, some of which was rather poor grazing land. And much of the weather encountered was less than ideal, with long stretches between suitable watering holes, which hadn't been predicted.

These factors put a noticeable strain on the herd, and Jake was beginning to entertain some doubts about this venture he had mortgaged his ranch to finance. The thought of going into winter with almost three hundred head of tired lean cattle was not an encouraging one, especially with the signs he'd detected of an unusually early winter, and he thought about his enormous investment and debt. His work ahead of him was going to be a challenge, and he held no rosy delusion to the contrary.

And there was the whole matter of his daughter's circumstances to think about. He had plenty of time to think about it out in the open country, but he hadn't even had a chance to talk to her yet since he'd been home.

After all of his contemplating he came to the conclusion that, regardless of what he might think to say to her about what she'd done, and regardless of what he thought about it, it was impossible to reverse her situation. Things were as they were. She would live with the consequences of it all, and hers could be a mighty awkward future without a husband. He decided that, now more than ever she'd be needing her father's support.

It was time to have a talk with her. They'd always had a close father-daughter relationship, and even when their lives were turned in new and different directions, that shouldn't change. She grew up like a son to him in many ways. Initially he even considered bringing her along on the cattle drive, because she was good with animals and a skilled rider. But that was before he was aware of her situation, and he had already decided that Mrs. Rhodes would need assistance looking after the ranch and the daily chores while he and Stew were away.

After he and Stewart got every head counted and the gate latched, he splashed some well water in his face to rinse away some of the range dust, and then went inside to talk things out with Emily.

Mrs. Rhodes intuitively understood their need for some lengthy private dialog, and she grabbed up two skillets and a pot and wandered out to the well with a scrub brush and a drying rag, leaving the two alone in the kitchen.

"Ann says I'm going to be a grandpa pretty soon." Was all he could think to say initially.

Emily stood close to the fireplace, watching water in a pan over some coals, waiting for it to boil. She was convinced in her own mind that her pregnancy was beginning to show, but she wasn't sure how obvious it looked. She felt self conscious about it, and she hadn't known exactly what to expect of her father's reaction to the whole affair. She certainly hadn't expected those words, but as she thought about it, she realized she could have expected that he would take the most optimistic view of the situation. That was typical of him. And she suddenly felt as though a huge burden had been lifted off of her.

He sat down at the table, and she turned to look at him. She could see the weary look in his eyes from the long days of moving cattle across all kinds of terrain.

"Would you like your pipe and tobacco?" She offered.

"Yes, I would really like that." He said. "I don't know how I missed packing it with me, but I sure wished I had my pipe out there in the evenings in camp."

She brought him his favorite pipe and his small tin of tobacco, and then sat down at the table herself while he lit the end of a thin piece of wood over the candle on the table, which he always used to light his pipe with. They had a lot to talk about, and they knew they would be talking for awhile. They both felt more at peace with everything than either had in weeks, and both were thoroughly glad that he was finally home.

"It looks like you'll be a grandfather in the spring." She said.

Not everyone had the clairvoyance to forecast the sort of winter that was in store for the region. The Haskins obviously hadn't expected it, and neither did Jacob or his banker. If there had been any such expectations, this whole cattle business venture would surely have been on hold at least until spring. An early deep frost followed by a heavy snowstorm gave them all some indication of what lay ahead.

By early November a fluke blizzard was sweeping across the foothills and covering everything in sight. Jake and Stew found themselves fighting against nature's fury to save the horses, cattle, and the few sheep and goats on the ranch, working through the worst of it and desperately braving the dangerous conditions to find strays in the blinding whiteness, pulling them out of snow drifts, and coaxing as many as possible to shelter. The barn and other structures would only hold so many animals, however.

But the wind kept blowing, and the temperature kept dropping, keeping area ranchers scrambling to save their livestock. And keeping that many animals properly fed was also becoming a challenge as the days progressed without the snow melting. They'd stored up some hay, but not nearly enough to handle such unusual and extreme conditions. Some of the animals didn't survive the cruel conditions.

After only the first few weeks of winter the loss to the herd was already greater than Jacob's acceptable margin. If things didn't start turning around real soon, he worried, he'd have big troubles by spring. He was no longer thinking so much in terms of profits, but now just hoping things would hold so he could break even on the deal and keep the ranch out of foreclosure.

That was still months away. He realized that a lot can happen in a few months, not much of which could be expected to be particularly beneficial in this kind of weather. But in the face of everything, he tried to remain optimistic. He was going to maintain his vigilance over his investment with every drop of sweat he had.

A second crisis arose when Emily, whose health had been worrying Mrs. Rhodes for days when her spirit appeared much lower than usual, finally came down with a dreadful fever. The housekeeper tried every remedy she knew, but wasn't able to bring the fever down. She feared the girl's life would be in grave danger if something wasn't done quickly to bring her out of it, and she explained her diagnosis to Jacob.

For Jacob, all the cattle in the world and all the ranches in the west were close to meaningless if he were to lose his little Princess, so he left the affairs of the ranch in the good hands of Stewart and Mrs. Rhodes and rode his horse through the miserable weather conditions to find a doctor.

Whenever anyone needed a doctor in these parts, it was usually for something serious. Country folk relied heavily on their own family remedies for the most common ailments. But on those rare occasions when a doctor was clearly needed, none were considered more knowledgeable than Dr. Warren Lukehorn, who, unlike most of the practicing local doctors, had impressive credentials from the most respected medical schools back east. He was viewed as rather arrogant and a bit eccentric, but as far as medical doctors this side of the Rocky Mountains were concerned, he was considered the best.

After a considerable ordeal, Jacob found the doctor and persuaded him to ride back with him to the ranch. Dr. Lukehorn initially resisted his pleading, stating that he had too many dependent patients in town to risk wandering off to the foothills where the drifts were rumored to be deep in some areas. He explained that it would be irresponsible, as it would divert his attention away from too many other concerns where his expertise was regularly needed, and it would simply be too risky.

But Jake hadn't come all the way to town in such nasty conditions just to turn back for home without a doctor. He was convinced that Emily's illness was an urgent matter that required the immediate attention of a qualified doctor, and he stubbornly persisted with his request until the doctor relented. He had to endure the doctor's annoying complaints about the biting wind all the way to the ranch, but he was grateful beyond words for the employment of his services.

When they arrived, they found Emily's condition at its worst that it had been up to that point. Dr. Lukehorn opened his medical bag and removed several tiny bottles containing various treacles, and set them on top of Emily's vanity where he could read the labels. Then he directed Mrs. Rhodes to heat up a pan of water, and bring him some wash cloths. When he checked her temperature he discovered the severity of her fever, and he realized the challenge he faced.

"How long has she been like this?" His question had a hint of worry in it.

"She's been in a miserable way for several days," Mrs. Rhodes explained "but I think she's been in and out of the worst of it. She was awake for a time yesterday, and then she woke up a few times in the night. She moaned frightfully, the poor girl. I do hope we're not too late bringing a doctor out here."

"Does she have any other conditions you're aware of?"

Mrs. Rhodes hesitated before answering. "She's with child. You don't suppose that has anything to do with this, do you?"

The doctor didn't comment immediately. He wiped away the perspiration from Emily's neck and face with the steaming wet rag handed him as she stirred restlessly, still unconscious. He couldn't help noticing how attractive she was, even in her current state of ill health.

"Where's the husband?" He finally asked, ignoring the question asked him.

"He's in the mountains prospecting for gold."

Dr. Lukehorn looked at Mrs. Rhodes with surprise. "In this weather?"

"It was summer when he left." She said.

"When is he expected to return? A man should be aware of his wife's condition, if he doesn't already know."

"We cannot be certain that he *will* return, Dr. Lukehorn. He apparently told her that she would see him before the end of August. But she hasn't seen him since he left the ranch in June. We don't even know whether or not he's alive. A lot can happen to someone in the mountains."

The doctor shook his head in disgust. "A tragic story indeed."

"Do you think you can help her, Doctor?"

James Ballou

He poured a liquid into a measuring beaker and held it up in front of a candle to determine the exact dose. "Her symptoms suggest pneumonia, which is certainly very dangerous. But I shall administer the best modern medicine, and she is young and appears to be otherwise normally healthy. I would say that her chances for a full recovery should be quite good."

Feeling that he'd done all that he could do for his daughter, and trusting that she was now in expert care, Mr. Thibault left the warmth of his house to tend to his weakened stock.

It was snowing hard in the mountains when Milton breathed his last breath. Nathan knew the very instant the life had relinquished the tired old man's body, as there was a quiet stillness about him, and the look of tension that had lately become so familiar to him had completely vanished from his face.

Conditions outside for digging a hole in the ground to bury him in probably couldn't have been much worse. There was close to two feet of fresh snow over almost a foot of crusty ice, and the earth just beneath all of that had already frozen hard. The old man had been proven right about the sort of winter conditions settling into the region. Everything about the storm seemed extreme by California's standards.

But Nathan didn't want to wait out the storm. There was no way to predict how long it might last, and he didn't want to leave a dead man's body inside the shelter any longer than necessary, or even outside in the open where coyotes or wolves might gladly feed on his carcass. Even if that didn't happen, the way the snow was falling he'd have to dig through it to find the body later just so he could bury him again, and it would take more digging later. He decided that it would be better to get it done as soon as he could. He cloaked himself in a thick wool coat and leather gloves

154

and his hat, and grabbed a shovel and a pickax for the task before him.

After selecting a spot near the old man's garden, but on higher ground overlooking it just as Milton had requested when he was still alive, Nathan began chipping and digging as huge snowflakes found their way through the tall pines, rapidly accumulating and making it difficult to gauge his progress. But he kept hacking into the cold hard ground, through stringy tree roots and all, eventually excavating an oblong hole nearly four feet deep.

He rolled his friend up in his best Witney point blanket and carefully set him in the hole before it could fill in with too much snow, and covered him over with the earth of the land he had made his homeland for the last twenty years of his life.

Nightfall was converging on the snowy Sierras as the final scoops of dirt were shoveled over the grave. Nathan felt physically exhausted, and after the job was done he stood silently staring at the snow-covered ground, paying his last respects before retiring to the shelter of the cave.

He had erected a hasty structure with a roof and side walls thatched with pine boughs tall enough to shelter his mule when he saw the first signs of the storm coming, and while it shielded the animal from snow and wind on three sides and above, it wouldn't be warm enough on the really cold nights he predicted. He'd learned that the water supply, the natural spring tricking water from the hillside, had frozen solid the night before, and it felt like it was getting colder on this night already.

There wasn't an abundance of space within the cave for an animal the size of the mule. He wouldn't have much room to move about. But as a temporary emergency shelter to keep warm in, it would have to do for the night. Nathan was also conscious of the fact that the mounds of grass stalks he'd collected before the big snow to keep the mule fed were rapidly being consumed, and it would be awhile before fresh vegetation would again be accessible.

The mule seemed reasonably content to endure the claustrophobic atmosphere of the cave, partially to escape the conditions outside, but Nathan understood the bigger reason was to escape the loneliness out there. And Nathan was beginning to feel a nagging sense of loneliness himself. This was Milton Galley's home, but the old mountain man was no longer around.

As he gently combed the ice clumps and pine needles out of the animal's main, he thought about how much lonelier he would be right now without his mule. Nathan's blankets were draped over the guest bunk where he'd slept a number of nights during his stay on this mountain, but close to the opposite wall was Milton's empty bunk, where the ailing old timer slowly surrendered his ghost after a long struggle. It was strangely hard to stay here with him gone.

And it was occurring to him more and more that he was long overdue in fulfilling his promise to return to Emily. He'd been missing her all along, but hadn't found the proper occasion to leave the mountains. But everything was different now. There was nothing to keep him in the mountains even another day. He decided to ride through the deep blanket to Placerville in the morning, where he could get a haircut, shave, and a bath, and maybe buy a new clean shirt, and then head directly from there to the Thibault Ranch.

The first person Emily saw when she woke up was Dr. Lukehorn, sitting on a chair next to her bed, watching her closely. As she had never seen him before, she had no idea who he was, or even that he was a doctor initially. She felt completely disoriented and confused at first, only gradually coming to the conclusion in her mind that he was a doctor there to treat her illness. She felt tired, but her fever was gone. She wondered how long she had been in an unconscious state.

"How do you feel now, Emily?" He asked.

"Are you a doctor?"

"Yes, I'm Dr. Lukehorn. Perhaps you've heard of me."

"No, I don't believe that I have. Is my condition serious? How long have I slept?"

"You've had a nasty feverish spell. If I hadn't come out here with my advanced remedies, I am certain your condition would now be much worse than it is. How are you feeling now?"

"I do feel weak. I would like to see my father. Is here around?"

"He is currently tending livestock, but I expect he'll be in after awhile to check on you. He's been very worried about you, as has Mrs. Rhodes."

"Am I going to be well?"

The doctor nodded. "I am optimistic. You are young, and I have solid confidence in the medical practices I administer. But you'll need to do your part, and get plenty of rest and nutrition. We are concerned about your well being, as well as your child's."

Emily felt embarrassed, being unaware that Dr. Lukehorn believed she was married. But she was also worried about the well being of the child she carried, and she felt grateful to be under a doctor's care with her current condition being what it was.

When the doctor finally discovered that she was in fact not married, he uttered some almost indiscernible comment of contempt for the irresponsible drifter who'd left her in such a predicament. She wanted to defend Nathan's position, but couldn't think of anything to say except that she wished he were there with her at that moment. She seemed to be the only one in the room who held onto any hope for Nathan's return.

Of the number of strays Jacob and Stewart pulled out of snowdrifts, few were found alive. Conditions had been severe during the previous nights, and a devastating blow was delivered upon an already beaten up herd when temperatures dropped to their lowest thus far, falling to well below zero during the coldest nights with blizzard conditions. The majority of the animals had previously only experienced the warm climate of the south, and the current environment was unusual even here. It had a drastically disorienting effect upon much of the herd.

By now he was seriously regretting having made the investment, knowing full well that it would take something close to a miracle to save them from financial ruin. But he worked on, trying to convince himself that he wasn't struggling completely in vain. It challenged every optimistic bone in his body.

It was usual for Jacob to confide in Stewart about matters he was normally careful to not trouble others with. He'd known him perhaps longer than he'd known anyone else now around, and he'd come to rely on him in no small part for his common sense. Mr. Bell wasn't well educated in academics, but he had a good head for sorting out the day to day concerns involving the ranch.

Jacob lamented after they'd discovered yet another frozen stray "At this rate, by spring we'll be lucky to have half the herd we started with. I've lost count, but it ain't lookin' good for us. I never thought I'd be sayin' this, but I'm worried. And I don't remember ever being this worried before about anything. It's not just the herd, but…"

"I hear ya, Jake. But no one could'a perdicted all what's happened. I keep thinking what you always said, that things always tend to work out for the best in the end."

"Well this time I'm worried, Stew. It'll take a miracle to get us out of this mess. And I'm 'specially worried about

Emily. She's too young to be this close to dyin'. The same sort of fever took her mother, remember?"

"Well, they say that Dr. Lukehorn is the best there is. You done all you could do for her, Jake. Some things we just have to leave up to the Almighty. You gotta have a bit of faith in somethin' b'sides yourself, when you're over your head in somethin'."

Jacob nodded. He knew Stewart was right. He had made some unfortunate decisions against unforeseen events all right, but while there would be consequences to his own errors in judgment, certain things were obviously outside the scope of his control. He could see no benefit to his anguish. He would have to yield some of his burden to a higher power, he admitted to himself, just to maintain his characteristically amiable disposition, if not his sanity. He had never been a regular church-going man. For Jacob, a sense of spiritual connection had always been a private kind of a thing. Right now he whispered a desperate prayer, noticed by Stewart only by the small fog of his breath.

Despite the misgivings expressed recently by some on the Thibault Ranch concerning Nathan Clayburn, Mr. Thibault still held out hope that the young man would make good on his promise to Emily and return to her, and that he would, like a respectable man, take responsibility for the child he'd fathered. For months there had been no sign of him, nor any word at all from him, but Jacob realized there could be a number of possible different reasons for that. Whatever they were, he wasn't ready to abandon his inclination to give Nathan the benefit of the doubt.

Just as the weather conditions began to take a turn for the better, Emily's health also started improving, and her strength returned gradually, diminishing any fears for the well being of the child she carried, as well as for her own survival.

As might be expected, the doctor received enormous praise and gratitude for his efforts perceived to have saved Emily's life, and no one could dispute that he was deserving of it, considering the care he'd given her with diligence, and the effectiveness of his medicines.

But what hadn't been perceived, not even by himself, was the degree to which he was already bewitched by her. Even as she recovered from her worst debility, her personality beamed with her natural attractiveness.

A man with thirty-eight years of age, the doctor was certainly old enough to be a father of someone Emily's age, but he had never married or fathered any children. The difference between them in age wasn't a big enough reason to prevent him from being hopelessly infatuated by her, and neither was the fact that she was pregnant with another man's child, now that he realized she was in fact not married. And it was a powerful infatuation he felt, though an emotion he was not so familiar with. He couldn't remember ever having the same kind of feelings before, at least not that he'd ever admitted to himself, or even allowed himself to entertain. Even now, he felt compelled to keep it to himself. After all, he was a professional man, and Emily was his patient.

But as her health improved, he found the prospect of courting her more and more tolerable to his sense of dignity, and he invited her to a play performance in Sacramento.

"Am I well enough to make the journey?" She asked him, automatically thinking she'd be riding her own pony.

"I think the entertainment would be beneficial to you, but you needn't worry about making the journey. I'll hire a coach."

A brief spell of warmer weather immediately followed the worst storm of the year to date, and the white ground covering began to recede, exposing more of the familiar countryside. The general expectation was that the winter conditions would return with a renewed fervor, but the mild conditions in the meantime provided a welcome break.

On a Saturday morning, only two days after he had offered the invitation to a play, Dr. Lukehorn showed up at the ranch with a horse-drawn Broughan carriage pulled by two horses, and driven by a well dressed man (for cold weather) he'd hired to taxi Emily and him to Sacramento for an afternoon of entertainment at the Sacramento Theater.

She couldn't hide the fact that she was excited to see a play. That was always a rare treat for anyone growing up closer to the mountains than the city. For Emily, it was a privilege just to visit Sacramento. An afternoon of theater entertainment would make it a particularly special occasion. For Dr. Lukehorn, it was what he hoped would be the beginning of the courtship he was planning. He had decided in his own mind that Emily, in spite of her prior errors in judgment resulting in her becoming pregnant out of wedlock, would make a suitable wife for him. And given his standing as a respected doctor, he didn't expect anything less than complete gratitude and willingness from her for such an opportunity.

Emily couldn't help being impressed by Dr. Lukehorn. She had by now learned from Mrs. Rhodes that he was a well known and highly regarded doctor across several counties, in spite of his usual lack of natural congeniality. But what he lacked in certain estimable personality traits, he made up for with his skills as a physician, and just about everyone around knew it. And he had enjoyed a level of prosperity in his career that other doctors envied. While there was some truth to the rumor that he'd inherited a comfortable fortune, his passion had always been medicine, and he'd made quite a name for himself in his field. He was, by most locals' standards, considered well to do.

His presumptions were blind to the flame still burning in her heart for the man he had only heard about, however, and the comfortable lifestyle his profession could provide wouldn't be enough to extinguish that flame. His own egotistical arrogance would prevent it from making complete sense to him, but he was faced with the reality during their coach ride back to the ranch after the play, when he made his first move toward a more familiar relationship by putting his arm around her.

She hadn't expected him to make such an advance, and it completely caught her off guard. She made no immediate attempt to squirm free, mainly to avoid offending him, but she felt awkward, and she suspected the pale skin color of her face might have changed to something closer to beet red.

"I thoroughly enjoy your company, Miss Emily." He said, completely ignorant about how *she* felt. "I'm already looking forward to our next occasion together."

Her mind searched for words. "I am grateful to you, Dr. Lukehorn, for saving my life, and I enjoyed the play very much, but I should tell you that I…"

"Please call me Warren. Others may call me Doctor, but I'd rather you called me Warren."

"Very well, then, Warren. But have you forgotten that I'm carrying another man's child?"

"The fact that you are in such a way is a good reason alone that you should wish for a husband. That I happen to be a doctor can only be seen as an added benefit."

"But my heart belongs to the father of this child." She firmly stated. "I'm sorry, but I cannot betray my own heart."

He slowly drew his arm back, and remained silent for a lengthy pause, trying to make sense of the situation. She obviously believed she was still in love with that young man who left her like this, but that seemed completely foolish. Where was he now? If he felt about her the way she felt about him, why wasn't he here with her? Nobody seemed to know where he was. The only thing anybody knew for certain about him was that he wasn't with her now, and he hadn't even bothered to come around to see her for months. Eventually she'd have to realize that if he hadn't returned by now, it'd be quite unlikely that he ever would. But that would take some time, and the doctor could see that now. He felt confident that she would eventually see that the young man (that irresponsible young man) wouldn't be coming back. As more time passed by, it would become more and more evident to her. But that would be fine. The doctor could wait. He could wait because he was confident the young man was long gone, probably half way across the country by now. And the doctor had so much more to offer her.

"I understand completely, Miss Emily. But time has a way changing how we feel about things. Time is all you need. I'm willing to give you that."

CHAPTER X

Nathan was so eager to see Emily he couldn't think much about anything else. He'd acquired some new clothes and gotten himself thoroughly groomed and cleaned up. Now he was ready to see her, now that he looked smart and possessed actual financial resources.

He could feel his heart thumping with exuberance as his mule carried him onto the Thibault Ranch over patches of snow in the moonlit evening shortly after sundown. A few minutes later, his knocking at the front door was answered by Mrs. Rhodes, who appeared visibly surprised at the sight of him.

"Mr. Clayburn? Well, isn't this a surprise? We've all wondered if we would ever see you again. Please come in out of the cold. Emily will surely be surprised to see you. She is out right now, but I expect her to return anytime now. Please come in."

Her previous inclination to reprove the young prospector if she were to ever see him again suddenly gave way to a more gracious welcome upon seeing him dressed so handsome, and now realizing that he had returned to make good on his promise to Emily, even though he was several months later than promised. His reasons for returning so late would be divulged soon enough.

In the half hour or so following his arrival, while he sipped the coffee Mrs. Rhodes heated up for him, Nathan learned from her that Mr. Thibault had purchased a very large number of cattle and had already lost much of the herd in the terrible storm that no one would ever have expected. "A cruel disaster" was how she described it. And even now, with the subtle hints of a slight warming trend in the air, and after another overcast day had faded into evening darkness, the worried rancher was still outside working to prevent the loss of any more animals.

"He'll be coming in most likely within another hour – his usual time lately since the first cold snap threatened the livestock, and Emily should be home by then as well." She explained. "I'm cooking chicken this evening, and if my guess is accurate, you must be nearly starved after your journey getting here."

He picked up his coffee cup and nodded. "Your guess is perfectly accurate, Mrs. Rhodes, I am starved. I hope that my unexpected arrival does not create an inconvenience."

"Emily will be so surprised. And when she sees how handsome you're looking now, why… She has been quite ill recently, Mr. Clayburn. She had us all very worried for awhile, but she's been making a remarkable recovery. Oh, there is just so very much to tell. But I should leave the important news for her to tell. She will want to tell you herself."

The curious look on his face almost asked the obvious question without words. He stared at Mrs. Rhodes as if waiting for an explanation.

"Important news?" He asked.

Just then Mrs. Rhodes noticed through the kitchen window the two glowing coach lamps coming up toward the front of the house, and she could vaguely make out the silhouettes of the horses pulling the vehicle up the drive.

"They've returned." She said, with a certain excitement in her voice.

Nathan couldn't help wondering who she meant by "they". Perhaps Emily had been out helping her father, and it was the two of them returning to the house.

He followed the housekeeper to the front door to greet them, and there stopped at the front of the porch was the coach, and he watched as a finely dressed, sophisticated appearing man held Emily's hand while helping her out of the partially mud-covered contraption.

Even in the very limited light of the moon and the coach lamps, Nathan couldn't help noticing how Emily had changed since he'd seen her. She was far enough along carrying the child that it could no longer be hidden from anyone who'd known her before. And though he wished his eyes were deceiving him, he knew they weren't.

Suddenly everything seemed to confirm the obvious; Emily must be this other man's wife now, and that would certainly make for some "important news" as far as he was concerned.

He couldn't see any reason to stay around even a minute longer. He hadn't expected to see what he'd seen, and he didn't believe he could endure much more of it. Besides, his own presence would only create the most awkward atmosphere in the house if he stayed for supper. Emily was the reason he came to visit the ranch, but now he was convinced she was another man's wife, and already starting a family with him.

Emily first noticed that Nathan had come to the ranch when she caught a glimpse of him out of the corner of her eye as he was riding away on his mule. He had unhitched the picket rope and climbed into the saddle while Mrs. Rhodes thought he was still standing behind her in front of the door waiting to greet Emily.

Even in the night Emily recognized Nathan, and his mule. She was so completely surprised to see him she was utterly stunned at first, and then she began to run after him.

"Nate!!!" She cried "Nate, don't leave! This is not what it looks. Nathan, please!!"

But it was no use. He clearly wasn't coming back. She wasn't even sure whether he heard her calling out to him or not. He just kept riding, soon disappearing into the darkness of night.

By the time Mrs. Rhodes caught up with her she was weeping uncontrollably. She started behaving hysterically, which was not normal behavior for her at all, but not much about recent events would be characterized as normal. Mrs. Rhodes removed the tippet off of her own shoulders and wrapped it around Emily.

"You shouldn't be out in the damp evening air like this, girl. You've just recovered from a miserable ordeal, and you wouldn't want it repeated."

"Oh, Ann." Emily said between sobs "He saw me with Dr. Lukehorn, and he thinks…"

"He just needs time to think, that's all." Mrs. Rhodes interjected, trying to calm the girl down. She sighed. "This is my fault, really. I didn't get some things explained that I should have. I just wanted to leave the important news for you to tell, because it really is yours to tell. I had no idea he would run off before you'd get the chance. I am sorry." She held Emily in her arms close to her to comfort her. "He just needs time to think about everything. He'll come back, I'm sure of it."

But she *hoped* that he would return soon, more than being as certain as she sounded. The one thing she was certain about was that Emily needed something to hope for, and to believe in her heart. Lacking that, it would be too easy for her to fall back into that dangerous state of mental and physical depression, and her health and the health of her baby were much too important to allow that.

When Emily finally gained back most of her composure, she felt embarrassed about having created such a scene in front of the doctor and the driver. Mrs. Rhodes walked with her back toward the house slowly, giving her the time she needed to dry away her tears. But even when her eyes were finally dry, she still couldn't wash the tears away inside. The fact remained that Nathan was gone, and there was no reason to be sure that he was ever coming back.

He tried to get it all out of his mind. What he'd seen the night before made that especially difficult. He couldn't stop wondering how it could be. When he was with her in June he was thoroughly convinced that her heart was set on him, and he was sure he had never met a girl who seemed more genuine, or more determined to follow her own heart. So what could have happened in the months that followed to throw her off track?

He didn't want to believe it, but he had the answer to that question; that other man. That sophisticated, probably well to do gentleman whose hand she so graciously took hold of upon stepping out of the coach. There could be no doubt about the relationship there. She was clearly going to be having the man's child, the way she looked. There could be no mistake about it.

Nathan was feeling a mix of unpleasant emotions; deep sadness, emptiness, pain, anger. But he realized he had nobody to blame but himself. He promised Emily he'd return to her before two months had passed, and he stayed away much longer. It wasn't right to leave her waiting that long, without knowing where he was, or how he was getting along. It wasn't fair to her, and somehow he understood it all along. But part of that time he spent away was occupied with unforeseen circumstances, where it wasn't either possible, or appropriate in his opinion to return to the ranch. He had the desire to return, and fell asleep dreaming about it nearly every night since he left. But there were opportunities, and he neglected to seize them. No string of excuses would change reality, not even in his own wishful mind. He promised Emily when he would return, and he failed to keep his promise. Now it was too late to repair the mistake.

Another snow was coming. He could feel it in the air. It was a chill. His whole world was a cold, empty, miserable gray universe void of the excitement he initially brought with him to California. And the things the old timer had said about gold not bringing satisfaction to the soul were proving true. Nathan had riches now. He was in possession of a huge Spanish treasure, as well as knowing exactly where to find decent nuggets. He could file a prospector's claim and start up a big operation. There was a lot of wealth waiting to be harvested in that stream. A year ago all of this would have had him restless with excitement, but that was before he found Emily. Now everything seemed practically meaningless when thinking about living the rest of his life without her.

He knew he had to get his mind focused on something – anything besides Emily. There would be no way to get her back, and all the hours spent wondering and thinking about how things *could* have been, were hours wasted. She was already making a family with that other man. Nathan felt too depressed to be hungry for breakfast, though he knew he would eventually have to eat something. He'd have to get on with his life.

There was still an unresolved matter that he'd neglected to take care of. Those two outlaws who robbed him and tried to kill him were still out there, roaming free to wage their wickedness against unsuspecting folks. Nathan felt a certain responsibility to put a stop to their activities, mainly because he was aware of it, and because his own life had been spared miraculously in spite of their attempts to end it. Milton had convinced him to let it alone, but now his life would seem to have no higher purpose than to find these men and bring them to justice.

Nothing about hunting them down was expected to be easy. They were hard men who had survived as long as they had most likely because they possessed plenty of experience raiding and looting mining camps, robbing stagecoaches, murdering anyone who got in their way, and eluding lawmen. They could do that quite successfully out here, in the mountains where civilized law and order hadn't yet been able to effectively reach them. Add to all of that the fact that months had gone by since his own encounter with them, and it was clear that he would have a lot of work ahead of him.

His first order of business was to make himself more proficient with the weapons he would arm with. He considered himself a reasonably accurate marksman with any good rifle, but he had less practice with handguns.

Colt's Army revolver had good balance and pointed naturally. Only three cylinder loads had been fired out of it since he'd bought it, and it seemed to perform well enough, but that was three months ago, and he hadn't fired the weapon since.

Back at the cave Nathan found a ten-pound canister mostly full of gunpowder among the old timer's supplies, along with hundreds of percussion caps and a gallon pail completely full with forty-four caliber lead balls, for that heavy Dragoon revolver which now belonged to Nathan as the old timer had insisted before he died. The supplies in the cave included enough ammunition to last Milton two lifetimes.

There were other guns also left to Nathan. A small William W. Marston double-action six-shot pepperbox pistol, which looked to be about thirty-one caliber, was hidden away in an oil cloth, and those gigantic .69-caliber horse pistols hanging on the frame timbers. There was even a smooth bore musket with a shortened barrel that would appear suitable as a close range scatter gun, if for not much else.

Nathan spent hours familiarizing himself with these weapons, determining their capabilities, and figuring out the fastest ways to put them into operation when needed. He found his Army revolver to be the easiest to shoot and hit accurately with, followed closely by that Colt Dragoon. The Army, Model of 1860, was clearly a gunfighter's gun, capable of being drawn from a holster, aimed, and fired in a fraction of a second. And with a bit of practice, Nathan found that he could thumb back the hammer and get a second accurately-placed shot fired quite rapidly. Colt's Dragoon was more cumbersome, but also a bit more powerful he discovered, because its deeper chambers held half again more gunpowder. He learned that it could also be mastered with practice, and he understood why Milton liked carrying it. It was a hand cannon with six powerful charges ready whenever needed.

The old timer also left behind several pairs of elk hide moccasins. Although they were a bit small for Nathan's feet, they had enough stretch in them to be worn to fit. They would be the perfect footgear for hunting, because a hunter could move around in them without making too much noise. Nathan realized their advantage over riding boots in that respect, and saved them for his own use later.

The cave wasn't a place where Nathan cared to stay long. It seemed cold, dark, and lonely now, and there wasn't really enough room inside to comfortably shelter the mule for any length of time beyond a few hours. It would only serve as a temporary retreat.

Pursuing those outlaws across a vast and mostly lawless land was going to take time, and he knew it. And he thought a lot about where he should begin his search. It had been roughly six months since they robbed and tried to kill him, so there would be no horse trail for him to follow. And in that amount of time, the two men could very easily have traveled a thousand miles or more.

The only specific information he had on them after they left him to die was where they sold the mule. Perhaps he could go back there, he thought, and try to pick up their trail from that point. Surely there were others around Placerville who had had dealings with them, and who might remember something that would prove useful to him in his search.

In spite of the torch she still carried for Nathan and her stubbornly faithful heart, Emily began to convince herself that she was never going to see him again. She wanted desperately to go find him and explain everything, but she had no idea about where he had gone. For all she knew he may have left California altogether, and gone back home to Missouri.

Meanwhile, Dr. Lukehorn, or Warren, as he preferred to be addressed by her, was not prepared to give up his quest for her affections, and he came out to the ranch to see her regularly in the weeks that followed.

Emily found herself progressively confused as more time passed without seeing any glimpse of the man she longed for, while the doctor, for whom she held no deep feelings, was making himself ever more ubiquitous. The point he had made about the practicality of her eventually taking him to be her husband, began to almost make sense when she thought about her future, and the future of the child she carried. Perhaps being practical was more important than anything else right now, regardless of what her heart was telling her.

When enough time had gone by to where she was able to think more clearly, she was finally able to admit with reluctance the fact that she really didn't know Nathan very well at all. She had only spent half a day and a night with him, and she began to realize how completely unreasonable it was for her to believe she could know him well enough to be in love with him. What Ann had explained to her was making sense now, that it takes time to get to know someone well enough to share a true love.

What made much of this cloudy in Nathan's case was the way his personality had a way of convincing most of the people who met him that they knew him completely right away. And most of them knew they liked him. Even Emily's father, who possessed much the same qualities himself, liked Nathan the very instant he met him.

The doctor wasn't at all like Nathan, but perhaps she could learn to see his better qualities. Perhaps in time she could learn to have some feelings for him as well. She realized that if she could do that, it could be better for her. She gradually opened her mind to the possibility, and began relenting to his persistence and accepting many of his invitations.

And the more time that passed by without seeing Nathan, the more hesitant Emily was to turn the doctor away completely. At least he was showing a consistent interest with his continued perseverance, which was a lot more than what could be said about Nathan right then.

When the time came to where the doctor decided to make a formal request for Emily's hand in marriage, she politely informed him that she needed some time to think about it. And she had quite a bit to think about. Her baby was due soon, and she still hadn't completely recovered from a broken heart. The thought of being anybody's wife other than Nathan's was a difficult one for her yet, even though she knew the child would need a father, and Nathan

173

wasn't around to fulfill that role. She wanted to give him more time and discharge every last shred of hope that he might actually return, but she knew that was a long shot, and she wasn't sure just how long the doctor would wait for her to make up her mind.

She was certain she had never been so confused in her entire life, and she did as she had done hundreds of times before whenever she felt unable to make a decision on her own; she sought the advice and wisdom of Mrs. Rhodes.

"Warren has, I mean, Dr. Lukehorn has asked me to marry him, Ann. I don't know what to tell him." She explained, expressing her sense of dilemma.

"Well," Mrs. Rhodes noted "he *is* a doctor, and a well respected one. He is also visibly financially successful. Your child would be reared in a proper home, with both a mother *and* a father. I suppose you should feel quite lucky, really, if he is so interested in you, with your situation such that it is. And we sure don't want to hold our breath waiting for Nathan Clayburn.

"But perhaps the most important thing you should ask yourself is, do you love him?"

Emily didn't answer. It was precisely the question she'd been trying to avoid asking herself all along. Maybe there was a chance she could learn to love him in time, but right now she didn't feel the electricity she'd felt when Nathan was around. It seemed utterly impossible that she could ever feel that way about anyone else. But there had to be something more to life than just a memory of such magical feelings, she was beginning to convince herself. Some things are a matter of perspective, after all. If she opened her mind, maybe she could see something she liked in the doctor. He seemed basically like a decent man, after all. But marriage? That was a mighty big step to contemplate. She needed more time.

It didn't take Nathan very long to find some folks in Placerville who were able to recall the two scoundrels. The town had certainly seen its share of scoundrels over the years, but those two individuals were as despicable as any seen around in a long while, and they'd made some folks a bit nervous during their brief visit. Nobody was particularly sad to see them leave. Nathan endeavored to conduct a thorough inquiry, and before long he was able to formulate a pretty good idea about where they were headed when they left town. There was a degree of consistency to peoples' memories on that matter, as there had been a collective desire to make sure the two had indeed left town.

The manhunt sent him back up into the mountains where the snow was deep. The higher elevation made travel and living conditions more difficult for men and horses, but the rocks and the trees provided good cover for anyone hiding out, and the adverse winter weather served to help discourage all but the most zealous lawmen and bounty hunters. Chances were probably very good those two scoundrels were wanted for other crimes somewhere and figured these mountains would protect them.

Nathan traveled with ample food and supplies now. Not only was he in possession of a substantial fortune with which to purchase anything he might need, but now he had hard-earned experience in the mountains of California. Now he had a better concept of what a traveler would need to get him through these mountains, and he was amply armed with guns and ammunition, and with his trusty mule to carry him wherever he needed to go.

Things were going to be a lot different this time. He was determined to learn the whereabouts of others in his area, before they had any clues about his presence. He would search hard for tracks, or signs of any kind, and travel as silently as he could. His campfires would be small, and situated where the smoke would disperse into the branches of trees. He would avoid crossing open fields or where the snow was deepest. And he would constantly be listening for sounds of horses or human voices. He would move slowly and observe the details of his environment. He would pay close attention to the chattering of squirrels, and the behavior of birds in the trees. He would listen to the sounds of the woods, and observe everything around him like he never did before.

It was several days before he spotted the first sign of an occupied camp. And when he did, he was able to approach within several hundred yards without being noticed, and from his position survey the better part of the campsite with the aid of the nautical telescope he had recently purchased.

There was a medium-size canvas tent set up on mostly level ground just above a year-round stream. The tent was apparently put up before the last heavy snow, because it was buried around the base, and the snow's surface was only disturbed around the entrance, which faced a different direction from where he approached. And through his lens he could see a thin screen of smoke arising from a stove pipe projecting from an opening in the roof of the tent, indicating that at least someone was inside trying to stay warm.

Nathan's approach was slow and cautious as he made his way on snowshoes toward the camp, careful to keep his own silhouette within the profile of the tall pine behind him, and to keep the early morning sun on his back. The soft snow provided an ideal condition for moving quietly – sounds were largely deadened by it. He had caught a glimpse of a horse's tail on the far side of the tent shelter, but whatever animals they had in camp wouldn't be able to see him from where he approached. But he knew he'd have to move silently and not waste much time if he was to get in without stirring them. His biggest worry was that his own mule, which was picketed some distance away, would start to fussing and alert someone to his presence. But thus far the animals had all remained silent.

His left thumb was curled over the hammer of his short musket, which he had loaded with an extra heavy charge of powder behind a big musket ball as well as a dozen thirty-one caliber balls, for a hefty "buck 'n' ball" load known to be devastating at close range. His right thumb was resting over the hammer spur of his Colt Army revolver, ready to rock it up and align the sights in an instant when the time came. The big Dragoon was tucked under his belt, loaded and ready.

He couldn't get the hideous images of those scoundrels' faces out of his mind, nor his memory of their brutality. He was prepared to see their faces again, possibly within just a matter of seconds, and this time he would have the drop on them. He wasn't going to let them get away with what they'd done. It was pay back time. He was completely ready to cut them down where he found them.

As he approached closer he heard the sound of voices within the tent, and laughter. There must be joke telling, and drinking. It would all come to an end very soon, he assured himself. Those scoundrels were going to be full of bloody holes and lead, and their days of robbing and murdering were finally going to be over.

He found himself filled with a new boldness as he now possessed the element of surprise, as well as enough firepower to fight the War Between the States all over again, it almost seemed. An instant later he found himself circling around to the front of the tent and swiftly entering uninvited through the door flap with his gun barrels leading the way. A surge of adrenaline rushed through his veins, but the risks surrounding such an aggressive entrance were overshadowed in his mind by his compelling need to right past wrongs.

One of the campers instinctively started to reach for a pistol tucked under his belt, but quickly decided against it when he saw the muzzle end of the short musket so close to his head.

There were three men in the tent not counting Nathan, and they were sitting at a small folding card table in front of a small stove. A nearly empty bottle of whisky and three tin cups sat on the table before them, and his sudden appearance found them dropping whatever hand of cards each held. None expected the game to end quite that way.

Hoping to avoid provoking him into pulling triggers, all three startled men slowly raised their empty hands to show they posed no immediate threat to their intruder, and remained silent and still, waiting to learn the true nature of this wild young man's intentions. There was a presumption that they were going to be robbed of any valuables they might have had, but they weren't anxious to agitate a man pointing cocked guns at them in such close quarters.

In the dim light he realized he had made a foolish blunder. These men were clearly not the scoundrels he had expected to find. He had never seen their faces before, but they didn't have the wild look of lawlessness in their eyes. They were older, perhaps in their late forties or fifties. And they surely didn't appear to be looking for any kind of trouble. There followed a lengthy uneasy silence while the men just stared at him, and then at one another, waiting, each dreading to make any move at all. Nobody seemed able to think of appropriate words for such an unexpected occasion.

"I see that I have just made a very terrible mistake." Nathan finally announced. "I've been trailing a couple scoundrels who tried to kill me, and I incorrectly thought... Anyway, I'll just lower my guns and peacefully remove myself from your camp. I only hope you'll accept my apology for the rude interruption."

He lowered the barrels of his guns and gently eased their hammers to the safe position, slowly backing out of the tent while he hoped none of them would seize the opportunity to grab for a gun. Nobody made any sudden movements while he could still see them, and once outside he awkwardly turned around, still wearing his snowshoes. He couldn't remember a moment when he felt more embarrassed, or more foolish. And it occurred to him only now just how hazardous his actions could have been, not only for himself, but for those other three men as well. Suddenly the old timer's wisdom about the foolhardiness of revenge began to make some real sense.

"Hey, Mister." He heard one of them calling from within the tent. He turned around just as the man stepped outside. "Say," the man asked him "have you had anything to eat?"

"Sure. I've got my own provisions."

"Well, would you like a drink, then?"

"Thanks for the offer, but I never acquired much of a taste for whisky, if that's what you mean."

"Well, all right. But cards are easier to play with four people. Better with even numbers, you see. You're welcome to stay here for a spell if you want to. That stove keeps the tent mighty warm. This is a good camp. Lots of fresh water in the stream. And it's full of hungry fish. They're not too big, but they're easy to catch. And we shot two deer before the last heavy snow, so we've got venison to spare."

"I'll have to talk it over with my mule." Nathan said, surprised by the man's hospitable invitation after his own careless intrusion. "See what he's got to say about it."

The man smiled. "Yeah, check with 'im. Make sure he understands we're tired of trying to play cards with only three."

179

CHAPTER XI

The three campers befriended Nathan, and he quickly established his opinion that they were all decent fellows. And they had come into the mountains, he learned, to prospect for gold, though they had yet to recover any. As one of them pointed out, this was a good location for a camp, but not particularly mineral rich. They had plans to move upstream in a couple of days and try their luck again.

In the meantime, they settled for card games and keeping warm by the stove, only getting out when it was necessary to tend to their horses, collect and split firewood, and hunt and fish. They had camped in this same spot for two weeks already, and now were beginning to run low on whisky. They'd have moved their camp a week ago had it not been for the heavy snow. They decided to stay put for awhile and wait for more agreeable weather, when the snow wouldn't be quite as deep as it currently was.

The experience level of these men, either as prospectors or mountain men, was the subject of some doubt in Nathan's mind. Just as it was with him when he first arrived in California, they didn't know where gold could be found, or, if any was actually here, they apparently hadn't mastered the methods of recovering it. And considering how easily he was able to walk into their tent and catch them all off their guard, he couldn't help wondering just how much wilderness savvy the three actually possessed between them. To their credit they had successfully hunted and fished, and they'd made a comfortable camp. But this could be a hostile land, home to outlaws, bears, and Indians. These men, for the most part, seemed unconcerned about the potential dangers of their environment. It was this same kind of careless disregard for security that very nearly got him killed last summer. His own act of invading their tent could also be considered careless, he realized after reflecting on it, for if they had been a bit more alert, he could easily have been killed right then. But at least he could see that now. He had a sense of the risk. Out here a man needed to have a sense of the risks, and keep himself vigilant if he aimed to stay alive. He wondered if these men had that kind of sense. He knew from his own past experience that they could find themselves in serious trouble without it.

Regardless of their experience, or lack of it, he liked them. They were friendlier than he could have expected, after that awkward initial encounter. And he enjoyed their company enough to spend some days at their camp.

While he camped with them he managed to find some time to reflect on recent events, and it started him on reconsidering the course he had taken, and got him thinking a lot about the nature of his motivation. And the more he contemplated things, the more it seemed like he was on the wrong course. It wasn't what he'd come all the way to California for. Now it was beginning to seem like more of a distraction than anything else, and not a very beneficial one.

Thoughts of Emily kept creeping into his head, though he tried hard to avoid them, knowing that no good could come of them. Her course and his own had obviously branched apart. The sooner he could accept that and forget about their short time together, the better it would be for him he knew. He couldn't change the way things were. But forgetting everything between them was only possible some of the time. She had left him so moved that forgetting her completely was going to take years, if it was going to ever be possible at all. That was how he was feeling about it, so he tried not to think about her. Whenever one of the men spoke of his wife back home, as occasionally one or another would do, it got Nathan to thinking about Emily all over again, before he knew it.

The more time he spent in the company of the unsuccessful prospectors, the more he learned to trust them. These were not men who wanted to cheat anyone of anything, but had simply come to the mountains each with a certain need to fulfill. And he understood it, because it had been the same with him.

And then an idea started to come to him. These men, being decent and honest men, were men he could trust. And he thought about starting up a prospecting operation up there on that creek where the old timer showed him where to consistently find good nuggets, and he knew that with the four of them, they could recover a handsome some. So he shared his ideas with them.

Initially they weren't convinced that he knew of a place where thumb-sized nuggets were an occasional find, and where pea-sized nuggets could be expected in every pan, as he was claiming. But when he poured a handful of nuggets out of a small pouch, they realized he knew where to find it. It was more than any of them had ever found. Indeed, more gold than they'd ever seen at one time, most likely. And they all agreed to participate in the prospecting operations he envisioned, which he was certain could make them all wealthy if they worked diligently.

The next morning they broke camp and packed up for the journey to the stream Nathan was talking about. It would be several days of travel, due to the nature of the terrain. But by now Nathan had learned a great deal of the Sierras, and he was familiar with some of the trails. He knew the best route to take.

The start of their prospecting operations were begun on Old Timer's Crick, as Nathan called it, as the mountain snow had only started to thaw in the early part of 1871, with just two sluice rockers and three gold pans. Nuggets were indeed found, just as Nathan had promised, but not without plenty of hard effort in the icy stream. It soon became apparent that a more productive apparatus could be erected and the current directed through it, which could wash more material in a given length of time than was possible with their present methods and equipment. Such an apparatus, because of its size, would have to be built at the site. Certain items of hardware they didn't have in their possession would be almost essential to the design the four of them finally came up with, such as wire screen, hooks, staples, nails, and the like. Their plans ultimately detailed a 15-foot stationary Long Tom sluice containing more than two hundred baffles in its floorboards to trap gold.

Nathan and one of the others set out for the little hardware store in Placerville to acquire the needed materials. They took one of the pack horses to haul a portion of the load, which would consist partly of other provisions they were running low on, including grain for the horses and flour, dried beef, hard bread, cheese, corn, and other food staples for themselves. And also, of course, more whiskey.

The hardware store was their first stop. And they were gathering up what they had come to buy when Nathan thought he'd seen the store clerk before. The man had a strangely familiar look, but Nathan didn't immediately place him. Having been in California less than a year, the man wasn't likely someone he'd known from a long time ago, unless he was a fellow Missourian, which didn't seem very likely.

He was content to dismiss this feeling he had, until he heard the man speak. The sound of the clerk's voice, and his way with words gave him away, and Nathan recognized him at that point. The man had cleaned himself up a lot, and gotten a shave and a haircut, but there could be no mistaking him now.

Without waiting to find out if the clerk knew who he was, Nathan dropped the cotton sack of nails to the floor and pulled his Army revolver from his belt and brought it to eye level, taking aim on the store clerk's forehead. The whole store suddenly went dead quiet except for the sound of the gun hammer slowly ratcheting back. The clerk showed no gun, but stared down the barrel with terror in his eyes, unable to move a muscle.

"Your name is Leroy, isn't that right?" Nathan asked.

"Leroy Mc….Canney. McCanney." He stuttered nervously. "Er…ya gon' shoot me, mister?"

"You and that Clive fella robbed me of all my possessions, and then tried to kill me up by my camp. Remember that? Where is he now, your partner, Clive?"

"He's dead. We wuz fixin' ta do us a bank in Sacr'menta 'few munts back, but thangs done gone real bad and that Clive, well, he got his self all full o' lead. Died right there in front o' the bank.

"They had me lock'd up after that, but Mister Hatley what owns this here store got 'em ta let me free, an' give me this job an' all, on account I once saved 'is life."

"Makes a fine story, but I aim to see you go back behind bars where you belong. I'll drag you back there myself if I have to, to see justice done. You should've killed me when you had the chance."

"Doncha reckon no one kin change, mister? Ain't it poss'ble 'ata man what did wicked deeds kin turn frum 'at manner o' doins? I did a heap a badness fer a long time, but I changed my ways. I knows I got sum payin' back ta tend.

I done wronged lots o' folks. Maybe cain't niver pay 'em all back, but a man's gotta make a try. Doncha reckon so, mister?"

"Justice would best be served by allowing this man to right his wrongs." A voice uttered from across the store.

A dignified looking gentleman appeared and approached closer toward where Nathan stood. He introduced himself as Frank Hatley, the owner of the establishment. Nathan didn't immediately lower his gun, or take his eyes completely off Leroy, lest he might make a fast move.

"Mr. McCanney has been an honest and faithful employee now for several months." The man stated in his clerk's defense. "I owe him a chance at an honest life, as he saved mine once. If you would make a list, my friend, of those possessions that were taken from you, I will do by best to fulfill it for you at no cost, if you will leave him be."

At that Nathan could no longer continue his threat, and he eased the hammer down on the revolver, and returned the weapon to its place under his belt.

"If he's really changed his ways, then I have no argument with him. I'm not here for trouble, but for nails and staples."

Nathan then picked the cotton sack full of nails up off the floor and set it up onto the counter. His partner, who had remained silent during the duration of the confrontation, followed him by plunking several bags up onto the counter also, ready to be weighed for purchase. The clerk wiped the nervous sweat off of his forehead with his shirtsleeve, and leaned against the inside of the counter to help support himself as his knees were too weak to hold him up for a moment. He didn't think his fear had been noticed, but Nathan noticed, and he understood it. He had felt the same way himself not so awfully long ago.

Nathan was now free from distractions. He could get back to doing what he came out west to do, and he had his mind made up. There was nothing left for him to do now but prospect for gold.

He no longer needed to find his fortune. He had already done that. And much of what had occurred in recent months now suddenly seemed almost unreal, as if it had all been part of a dream. But he was anxious to separate himself from his recent past, and get on with his enterprise and exploration.

He spent some weeks with the others, working closely with them in the frigid stream, eventually recovering a fair amount of rich nuggets and plenty of flake gold. It was adding up to an impressive hoard before long, which all had agreed to divide evenly by weight between the four of them.

When everyone was satisfied they'd made a sufficient harvest and the time had come for them to pack up and head for home, they set about to divvy the pot. Each man would return to his family with a newly acquired wealth of respectable size, giving himself a decent new start in life. The mood was generally high. Only Nathan seemed a bit sad in his mood that the enterprise had reached its end, and he'd be saying good-bye to his new friends, whose company he'd come to enjoy very much.

As it turned out, the others, being grateful to Nathan for letting them in on this precious secret, and trusting them enough to show them the rich stream, mutually decided to deduct ten percent from each of their three shares and add that to Nathan's. He argued against the plan, knowing that these men had families to provide for. Besides, he already had a sizeable fortune of his own. But they would not be dissuaded. Nathan wound up with more gold than he had ever imagined he would see in his lifetime.

After the others departed the area, he returned to Milton's grave, and spoke a few words. He had a feeling the old man could hear him, wherever he was now. But even if he couldn't, saying a few words made him feel a little more settled about things, and perhaps a little less lonely. Later on he couldn't even remember what words came to him to say.

Remembering what Mr. Thibault had said about the benefits to a man for planting his roots somewhere and settling himself down got Nathan thinking a lot about that now. There was nothing for him back in Missouri that he wanted, so he had no desire to return to that part of the country. And living high up in the mountains, while enchanting in the short term, could be a hard journey for extended periods, just as Mr. Thibault said, especially during the winter months. But the idea of a homestead in the foothills appealed to him, and now he possessed the financial resources to obtain in.

The first thing he would need to do, he finally decided, would be to establish his financial standing by opening a bank account. It could prove useful in the future if he ever needed borrowing credit, if for no other reason. He wouldn't have to yield the entire Spanish treasure, but only a portion as needed to secure his account with the bank. Milton's half was of course earmarked for the purpose he'd requested before he died, which was to help someone who was down on his luck. This would be Nathan's primary objective, to honor his friend, although he had not yet found that person who was in such straits.

The Bank of Sacramento was the logical choice for anyone in the region wanting to secure his assets. Any bank in a smaller town might be too vulnerable to robbery. Better to conduct business in the major settlements, he convinced himself. It just seemed that way to him, even if he couldn't think of a reasonable argument to back up his theory. The following day he was riding his mule out of the Sierras with as much gold and silver as he could fit into his saddlebags.

He looked ahead to running his own small ranch. In the past he'd worked on plenty of other ranchers' spreads, but never before imagined having one of his own. Now the opportunity was presenting itself for this to become reality, and he fancied the idea. He was no stranger to the hard work, but now he would be master of his own work, rather than doing it all for someone else's profit. He would have his own spread of land, and his own house, and his own livestock.

After some inquiring, he learned of a ranch for sale. And he found out that a neighboring ranch would soon also be for sale, because the owner, having fallen upon financial ruin, was unable to keep possession of his land. It was at the very moment he learned of these things that he was certain he heard Milton Galley's voice, and the words painted a clear picture of everything he'd heard. Even before he was told the name of the struggling rancher, Nathan knew what he had to do.

The sunniest, warmest day in months found Jacob and Stewart working to repair a section of fence, with birds singing in the trees louder than had been heard since the end of summer. Jacob's mind was filled with many different thoughts and worries, as was becoming a regular thing for him now, but today seemed different. At first he tried to imagine how different all of their lives would have been on the Thibault Ranch had Mrs. Thibault lived to see this day. In a very strange way, he seemed to be growing more peaceful within himself now, listening to the birds singing their songs of hope, and looking ahead to springtime, in spite of the unpleasant realities soon to be faced head on.

When they'd closed up the last broken section of fence with new slats and cross pieces, they started back toward the barn to return the tools. Stewart first noticed the coach approaching up the long drive pulled behind two horses, and he directed Jacob's attention toward it.

"Say, that the doctor comin' around to call on the little princess again, Jake? He sure comes around a lot lately, don't he?"

Jacob squinted his eyes for a harder look. "No, that ain't the doctor. Thatn's got lettering over the doors. That'd be Sam from the Sacramento Bank." He said with a dreading tone to his voice.

"What's he come all the way out here for, do you reckon?"

"Well, shouldn't be a mystery. I've had payments overdue on that loan. Haven't been able to make even a single one of 'em, what with all that extra feed I had to get, and not being able to get any animals to market. No buyers for these scrawny critters this year and all. Sure was hoping for a longer extension on my credit. But a bank can't hold things up forever, you know. Hell, I made a gamble, and I lost. Was real stupid, I'll admit, but there ain't a thing I can do about it now. I've never been sorrier about anything in all my life, Stew."

"Maybe he's gonna work with you on it. Maybe that's what he's come to tell ya. You've done business with him before."

Jacob shook his head. "He's already done give me plenty o' time, and he knows I can't make any payments this year. He wouldn't make this trip out here just to negotiate more. But he's just doin' his job. He works for a bank, not a charity."

They both just stood there waiting for the coach to come up and stop, which it did not more than twenty feet away from the well in front of the house. It was too early in the year for any visible dust rising off the ground behind it. This was a warm day, but the ground was still cool and damp.

A side door on the coach opened and the banker stepped out and stretched his legs. "Good afternoon, gentlemen." He tipped his small hat to them, then tried to straighten his suit.

"Afternoon." Jacob returned, perhaps less enthusiastic sounding.

"I sure am thirsty, Jacob. Mind if I get a drink from your well? I knew I should've carried a jug of water in the coach. Wasn't expecting so much sunshine today."

"Please help yourself, Sam. You'll find a cup or two there on a peg. But tell me truly, ain't it the bank's well now?"

Sam walked over to the well and took one of the cups off its peg, looking back toward his driver and raising the cup to offer him a drink. The driver shook his head, holding up his own small bottle of spirits. A series of turns on the handle of the axle raised the bucket full of fresh well water, and he dipped the cup and took a long drink.

"That tastes awfully good." He said after he finished swallowing. "I haven't tasted mountain spring water in years. Nearly forgot how good it is."

"It's never been a dry well, all the years I've been here." Jacob couldn't get the depressing thought out of his head that he'd have to leave this ranch he loved so much.

Sam removed his hat and wiped the sweat drops off his bald head with the handkerchief he took out of his pocket. He hadn't yet climatized to the unusually warm weather, but Jacob and Stewart perceived all of this to be merely stalling against the bearing of bad news.

"I'm being foreclosed on, ain't that right, Sam?" Jacob's patience was nearing its limits.

But Sam wasn't quite ready to give the answer Jacob was fishing for just yet. He put his hat back on his head and adjusted it, and looked up at Jacob.

"Now, that's something concerning what I came to talk to you about. But before I get to it, I thought you'd want to know about the Haskins Ranch, if you hadn't heard already."

"Cecil told me he was pondering putting his place up for sale. Cattle business was hard on everyone around here, I reckon. He decide to sell his place, then? Haven't spoke to him in some weeks."

"Already sold it. Seems like a kind fella, your new neighbor does. Suppose you'll be meeting him soon enough." Sam explained.

"So then, just how much time I got left here on this ranch?"

"The better question might be; how long do you expect to live?"

"What's that supposed to mean, Sam? You know, I always thought you were a straight talker. Always respected you for that. But you're doin' a lot of talkin' now that ain't real plain. I can't tell what you're trying to say to me."

"You're right, Jacob. Truth of it is, your debt with the Bank of Sacramento has been satisfied. Your ranch, your home, your cattle… It's all in the clear as of yesterday at Noon. You no longer owe as much as even a cent to my bank. I'm here to give you back the deed to your land."

"I don't understand. What are you talking about?"

"Well, it seems this matter of settling your score was in the will of a dying old timer who had a lot of gold. His dying request."

"Who was I to this 'old timer', that he'd do this for me? What was his name? Who was he? I can't think of anyone I ever knew that would…"

"His name was Milton Galley. He lived as a hermit up in the mountains. Was a prospector. Indeed, a successful prospector. To him you were someone in need. So that's what I came out here to tell you."

Jacob was almost speechless. "I, uh… I don't suppose you and your driver would care to stay for supper?"

"We've come this far. It would be impolite of us to refuse such an invitation. We mustn't be impolite. Besides, something smells awfully good. Still have that housekeeper? What was her name, Anita..?"

"Rhodes. Anita Rhodes. Yes sir, she's still with us. We all just call her Ann. Let's go on inside an' see what she's got cookin' already."

Emily gave birth to a healthy baby boy in the early hours on the last day of March, 1871. Her son was born at home on the Thibault Ranch, while Dr. Lukehorn was still on his way to the ranch after being summoned by Stewart, who'd made a midnight ride to the doctor's home. Throughout much of the journey, the impatient doctor repeatedly scolded his driver for failing to compel his team of horses to run faster.

She made the decision to name the boy Gabriel, much to Dr. Lukehorn's disappointment, to honor Nathan's wishes expressed that afternoon three-quarters of a year earlier, when he remembered his grandfather. Jacob let her know that he considered it a right fine name.

As soon as she felt up to it, she and the doctor discussed some of the details of the wedding they were now planning. She had by this time resigned herself, with much reluctance, to accept the doctor as her husband to be. She saw it as her only reasonable option at this point, considering all.

"As soon as that boy can walk and talk," said Warren "we should send him to one of the finer institutions on the East Coast. We'll have an obligation to make a gentleman out of him."

It was his occasional remarks hinting on sending her baby away at the earliest opportunity that frightened her most about the decisions she was making. She wanted to believe that he didn't really mean it, but she somehow knew he did, and that when the time came, he'd do just as he'd vowed. Her only hope was that before the boy was old enough to walk, his stepfather would grow too attached to him to send him away. But that was only a wishful hope she realized. It would be hard to imagine that aspect of Warren's personality.

Jacob grew increasingly curious about that old timer who'd saved him from financial ruin. The banker didn't have much information about him, and he explained that the details of the old man's will were to be kept confidential. The important thing, he reassured Jacob, was that the ranch was no longer at risk. Jacob was convinced that his numerous prayers had been answered. Who could have ever imagined that a dying old man, indeed a complete stranger as far as he knew, would take such a burden from his shoulders? He was convinced this had to be a miracle from heaven. He wanted to thank him for what he'd done, but he realized that would have to wait until he went on to the next world, wherever the old timer was now.

Things started turning around in early April. It was almost as if a plague had relinquished its hold on the region. The hard winter was dying down, and warmer days were growing longer and more frequent. The animals on the ranch, those that had survived the cruel months, were starting to look noticeably healthier and more active. The sun was out more often now, and the melting snow in the mountains sent gushes of icy clear fresh water into all the streams, and plants started turning green and full. Jacob found a new energy within him he didn't know still existed. His old self was coming back to life, and oh how good it felt. He was a man born again with a new start in life.

He hadn't yet met his new neighbor. Riding by one day with Stewart, he noticed some changes over there on the nearby ranch, but he had yet to see the young man whom now dwelled in the Haskins' old house. Pretty soon he would go over there and introduce himself, and make friends with the man. He looked forward to that, but he decided to let the man settle in some, and get his place organized to his own liking. Jacob had a feeling about this he couldn't explain. It was a sense about his new neighbor, whom he was certain he'd never met, or even seen before. But he felt he knew the unseen neighbor, and that he was a decent man. And it was almost a premonition he felt, that he and this new neighbor were soon to be close friends. Cecil was a fine man, and a good neighbor. The Thibaults and the Haskins had always gotten along well. But there was something different about the new rancher, which Jacob couldn't define because he had yet not even met him. Or so he thought.

The decision was final. Emily and the doctor were going to be married, and their wedding was planned for April the 8th, which was a Saturday. The service was to take place outdoors, under some trees just fifty yards from the Thibault's house on the ranch. Only half a dozen invitations were made. Keeping the event as small as possible seemed appropriate, mainly because of the baby.

Emily seemed especially curious about the new neighbor, whom none of them had yet become acquainted with. When she learned that he was not married and had no family living with him, she was intensely curious, and she was less eager to rush into the marriage with the doctor. Imagining what the new neighbor would be like made her think about Nathan, although that didn't really make a lot of sense to her. He could never be just like Nathan, no matter who he was. She started asking a storm of questions about the stranger, but her father only knew what he'd heard from the banker.

"Let the man settle into his new place a week or two." Jacob responded. "We'll invite him over for supper pretty soon. We'll get to know all about him then."

"I'll be Warren's wife by then." She said. "What if it turns out I should have waited a little longer to get married?"

"Well, that's maybe a reasonable enough concern. If you don't love him… Will he wait another month or two, maybe? I reckon you need some time to think this all through."

"No." She said. "Nope, he won't wait. He said it's got to be the date he set, or else I'll remain a single mother with a bastard child." She fought back the tears.

"Don't you worry about that, Princess." He assured his daughter. "This is a big ranch. It's a fine place to raise a boy like little Gabriel. He wouldn't have a father, maybe, but he'd have a granddad to teach him a lot of things."

"I know that, father. I can't imagine a better environment for a young boy growing up. And I can't imagine a grandfather a boy would rather have. It's just that I don't want him to grow up without both a mother and a father, who live as husband and wife."

Jacob thought about what she said, and it made perfect sense. She was right, the boy would need a father. He would need a regular kind of life that only a married couple could provide. And the doctor had resources, so Gabriel should never want for anything. She was right. But he couldn't stop thinking about how he'd always wanted a son of his own. Now he had a grandson. That was almost the same as having a son of his own. He could not have been happier, considering everything that had recently occurred. But he couldn't stand the idea of his little princess living in misery. He worried now about her future, but he knew he couldn't interfere with it. She would have to make her own decisions, based on her own convictions.

"I have to marry Warren." She said. "Gabriel will need a father."

CHAPTER XII

Nathan had moved onto the ranch he had purchased, and was beginning to make certain changes to suit himself. Most things were already to his liking, but he thought of a few changes he wanted to make.

A stone wall had been stacked between the garden area and a patch of woods, presumably to discourage deer from wandering in and eating the vegetables. But the wall didn't completely enclose the garden area, and it seemed useless unless it comprised a complete perimeter around the entire garden. Collecting and stacking enough rocks to enclose the garden would take a long time, but he had plenty of time. If it took several years to complete, that would be fine. He thought of making the larger part of it a picket fence, and use wood. That would be quicker to finish, but would require more work in the long run just to maintain. There were other fences on the property of the split rail type to contain livestock, and those just by themselves would be a matter of constant maintenance.

He made several trips up to Milton's cave to collect the rest of the guns, tools, silver and gold, and other items that might be of some value or use on the ranch. He rented two good pack horses from the same horse trader he'd dealt with previously. They'd developed a level of trust between them by now, and the man had the best selection of animals in the region, as far as he could determine.

The task consumed the better part of a week, as Milton had accumulated quite a collection of possessions over the twenty or so years he'd lived in the mountains, including a heavy iron anvil and a large box vise, as well as other miscellaneous blacksmith tools, hardware, and wrought iron stock. Nathan felt awkward stripping the cave of its contents, almost as if he were a thief raiding a tomb of its riches, but he kept reminding himself that he was simply acting on the old timer's wishes.

He knew that eventually he would be interacting with the Thibaults at some point, being their closest neighbor now. But he wasn't exactly sure just how that was going to feel. Common sense was telling him that his choice of location for settling down was the worst possible, considering his intention of getting Emily out of his mind. Had there been another ranch for sale in the same region but farther away, he was certain he would have given a lot of weight to these matters in making his choice. But the Haskins' Ranch was the only spread for sale in the whole Sacramento Valley. It was their place or no place, unless he wanted to build his own house on bare land, which he wasn't eager to do this year. This ranch was a very good ranch, and well worth what he had to pay for it. He was certain about that.

Weather conditions on the morning of the seventh gave an indication that the following day was going to be a nice one. There was no more snow on the ground at the ranch's elevation, and the sun had been shining most of each day for almost a week.

Nathan found the weather ideal for working outdoors, and he had some outdoor projects he was eager to get into. The stone wall was going to be a long-term project, but he also wanted to build a second chicken coup. He had most of the materials he needed for the job, but he was short on nails and spikes. Frank Hatley's hardware store was the closest to the ranch. A man could ride to it and back home to the ranch, he expected, in about a half of a day. He had some horses now, in addition to his mule, but he decided to ride the mule. He could sense that the mule was wanting to get out and go somewhere, as he sometimes liked to do lately. The horses seemed happy to stay behind and graze, on this particular day.

The little hardware store, being the only hardware store within miles, was starting to get busy with customers by the time Nathan arrived. The nice weather change from a hard winter found scores of farmers and ranchers out repairing fences, fixing roofs, felling trees, replacing wagon wheels, and preparing their soil for planting, among other chores. They needed tools, hardware, and various raw materials, and Hatley's store happened to be the most convenient place to buy what they needed.

Nathan plopped a canvas sack of nails onto a scale and watched the indicator rise toward the five-pound mark. Just then he heard a familiar voice speaking behind him, addressing him directly.

"'Scuze me, sir, ain't your name Nathan Clayburn?"

He turned around to see who it was and recognized him as the man who shod his mule last summer on the Thibault Ranch.

"Why, yes it is. And you would be… Stewart Bell, isn't it? You shod my mule that evening I spent at the Thibault Ranch, just last summer."

The two men extended their right hands for a respectful handshake greeting.

"What's got you here buying nails?" Stewart asked. "Sure been lots of wondering as to your well being, since last summer."

"Hope you'll pass it on I'm getting' along right well. Decided to go into ranchin'. Right now I'm fixin' to build an extra chicken coup. That's what the nails are for. What about yourself? What sort of task you got yourself into?"

"Repairing chairs for the weddin' tomorrow."

"Someone's getting married, huh? Anyone I might've met in that short time I spent at the ranch? Guess I only met four people, counting yourself."

"As a matter o' fact… Look, I know this ain't none of my business, but it seems a real shame that another man will be raising your son."

Nathan looked stunned. "I don't have a… Who are you talking about? Could you repeat that? Not sure I heard you right."

"Emily says he's your son, and the only reason she's tyin' the knot with the doctor is so's he can have a daddy. She don't love the doctor. That's what she says, anyhow. 'Course, none of this is any of my business. I don't like to nose into others' affairs. But you couldn't live there without knowin' plenty of what goes on."

"This is all quite a surprise to me. I had no idea." Nathan took off his hat to scratch the top of his head, contemplating everything Stewart just explained. "Figured she was already married to that dandy she rode with in the coach. Must've been that doctor you're talking about. Saw she was expecting. That was easy 'nuff to see. But I just thought… What's his name, this son of hers?"

"The doctor was staunchly opposed to the name she chose for the boy, but she insisted stubbornly and shc got her way on it. But like I said, he ain't just *her* son. He's your son just as much. That's what she'll swear to, anyhow. She named him Gabriel."

Stewart couldn't figure why Nathan hadn't shown up at the ranch by the time the wedding had started. He hadn't mentioned it to anyone that he'd seen him the day before at the hardware store. He didn't especially wish to pry into this whole matter and upset the way things were going to happen. He didn't feel it was his place to do that. He had lived on the ranch a long time without getting in the way of things there, and he'd be plenty happy living a good while longer the same way. But this seemed like a very odd kind of situation. Nathan seemed mighty concerned to learn he had a son, but where was he now, and how would he be able to let this wedding continue, knowing what he knows now? Surely he wouldn't want this wedding to happen, and he knew that it was planned for today, and he knew the time it was planned for. This wasn't making sense. Where was he?

Minding his own affairs was somehow more difficult for Stewart now, with everything he'd recently learned. Keeping his mouth shut was beginning to seem like an overwhelming burden all of a sudden. But then, what could he change anyway, he wondered, if he had decided not to remain silent about what he knew? Could he possibly have affected the outcome of things by wading in and saying something? Even if he could, the more important question might be, *should* he?

When the minister spoke the words, "If anyone should object to this union, let him speak now…" Stewart spoke. For the very first time in all of his years on the ranch, Stewart stepped outside the boundaries he'd set for himself long ago, and opened his mouth for the unthinkable purpose of interfering with the lives of others. But once he'd opened his mouth, he couldn't take it back. He couldn't pretend he hadn't said anything. He had blurted out the words, and now he would have to face up to them, right or wrong.

"I object to it. I object to this here weddin', which I don't believe was ever meant to be." He said, suddenly feeling all eyes focusing on him, demanding an explanation. "I object to anyone rushin' into sumt'n that changes a person's life forever, which ain't so easily reversed. Ain't sayin' it's any of my affair, 'cause I know that it ain't. But it wudn't hurt no one to give little Miss Emily a bit more time to ponder what she's doin'. That's all I'm sayin'."

There was a stretch of silence, then gradually folks began mumbling to one another. Finally the minister asked Stewart if he could provide a single good reason why the wedding should be stopped. He noticed a bewildered look on Emily's face, and the look of contempt in the doctor's eyes.

"All right, then." Said Stewart. "How about the fact that the father of her child ain't present. I ran into the young man yesterday in Hatley's hardware, and he learned right there for the first time that he has a son. I reckon the only reason he ain't here right now is on account he's on his way. I'd bet my last dollar that if he'd been here already, he'd surely object to this weddin'."

The doctor was noticeably infuriated. He always had next to no patience for anything that ever delayed his own plans even the slightest bit, and right now his impatience showed.

"Well," he huffed "he's not here now, is he? If he cared anything at all for this young lady to whom he has brought nothing but grief and heartache, he would most certainly have been here well before now, and begged her for forgiveness. But the fact of the matter remains that he is *not* here. Please, Reverend, let's continue with what we've all come out here for on this fine Saturday."

When Emily recovered more or less from her initial astonishment, she turned to Warren. "I wish to stop this ceremony." She stated firmly.

He seemed to be searching through his frustration for words to respond. "Oh my dear, we mustn't be thwarted by trivial speculations. Obviously the young man lacks any degree of interest. Let us waste not a moment longer concerning ourselves with him. We should return our attention to what we all came out here today for. Let us finish what we've started."

"I'm sorry, Warren," she persisted "but I cannot marry you. Until this point I wasn't able to see clearly, with wearisome matters lately troubling my mind. But I can see more clearly now, and now I know that I could never live with myself were I to betray my own heart. I'm sorry."

Dr. Lukehorn was more accustomed to his wishes being fully accommodated, and found himself unprepared for Emily's sudden and unyielding dissent. His face turned red with anger and humiliation, but he knew enough to keep his temper restrained in the company of others, hoping to avoid making a spectacle of himself. He stammered a bit, but quickly realized there would be no changing her mind. In an effort to salvage his dignity, and before he lost his composure, he summoned his driver and excused himself from the company of the Thibaults and their invited guests, departing as composed as his mood would permit.

As she watched the doctor's coach move down the long drive, she realized she had just closed a door she had desperately tried not to close. He may not have been someone she would ever, or could ever love, but he offered one thing – one very important thing out here in the still mostly wild west, and that thing was security. She threw that away when she dissented. She knew he wasn't going to return. This was a door now closed, and it would never again be opened. That was something she could be sure of, knowing the doctor.

To add salt to the wound, there was no sign of Nathan. Though she strained her eyes to scan the horizon, hoping he was out there somewhere riding onto the ranch, she knew it would be too good to be true. She could see nothing that even remotely resembled a lone rider, approaching from the far reaches of the huge ranch. Nothing out there appeared that could be distinguished from a tree, and the trees weren't moving.

She turned to Stewart, who was by this time having serious second thoughts about the situation he'd caused. What if he'd been wrong about Nathan, and the young man decided never to show his face on the Thibault Ranch again? That would leave Emily in a terrible state for some time. He thought about her being married to the doctor, and that scenario suddenly didn't seem nearly as terrible as it did previously, considering everything.

"Stew." She said. "You forgot to tell me that you saw Nate yesterday. Why'd you forget to tell me, knowing well enough how interested I'd be in knowing?"

"Same reason I shudda kept my mouth shut just now. Was afraid a causin' sumt'n like I just done. A man ought to keep such things to his self, and keep hi'self free of others' affairs. Doin' that always kept me outa trouble b'fore."

"Well, it's too late for that now, isn't it?" She remarked. "Where is he now, and why isn't he here? Didn't you tell him what was planned for today?"

"I told him. But you're askin' me why a man does what he does, and that's a mighty big question. Ain't always certain why I do some of what I do, like opening my mouth here t'day about me speakin' to Nathan yesterday. I reckon we can all see now that it weren't real smart. But every man has his own reasons for what he does, and Nathan's got his."

His words left her questions unanswered, but she knew he wasn't going to provide her with more. She knew Stewart well, and she knew he wasn't a man who cared much for making assumptions concerning other people. She could pester him with questions for the rest of the day, and end up knowing nothing more than what she knew right now.

As much as she wanted to prevent her emotions from showing, she could hold back her tears no longer. The knowledge that Nathan was aware of the wedding but failed to show up to stop it was more troubling to her than she would have expected, and it seemed to hit her all of a sudden. Nothing about it made any sense to her. Though she'd only known him for the duration of a single day, and that was three quarters of a year ago, they had connected in that short time. And it was a powerful connection she was certain. She could not understand why he wasn't present. It just didn't make any sense. No, she thought. It wasn't simply that he had decided not to show up. That would not be possible. No, there was some other reason. There was something outside of his control. Something was very wrong, and she couldn't hide her worrying, or hold back her stream of tears.

When Nathan awoke on the morning of April the Eighth, the biggest thing on his mind was the wedding they'd be getting everything ready for on the nearby ranch. He knew this was his last chance to talk Emily out of making the biggest mistake of her life, as he saw things from his own point of view. And he thought about everything Stewart Bell told him the day before; that she wasn't *really* in love with the doctor, and that her son was also his own.

He decided to get an early start, and get himself cleaned up after breakfast before heading over to the Thibaults' place. There would be plenty of time, but he was mindful of the consequences if he were late. Were he to arrive after the wedding was over, he knew it would be a mistake he would regret for the rest of his life. He'd already been living with a similar mistake, and it had been nearly unbearable. But now he'd been given a second chance. It seemed like a kind of miracle, but it was a second chance to get things right, and blowing it again would be unthinkable.

He wasn't worried. He still had plenty of time, and he couldn't imagine anything in the world that could possibly prevent him from getting over there before the wedding started.

He'd shaved his face, bathed in his tub filled with cool well water, and finally gotten himself dressed in his best freshly washed clothes to make himself presentable. He hadn't yet acquired a clock, so he stepped out onto his front porch to gauge the time as best he could by the position of the sun. It was still reasonably early he guessed, maybe eight o'clock at the latest. The air was still cool during that time of the morning in April, but he expected it to warm up quite a bit by noon. The earlier he could get over to the other ranch, the better, he decided.

Whenever he went anywhere he considered important, he preferred to ride his mule. He had developed a strange bond with the creature, and they seemed to understand each other amazingly well. None of his horses were quite as intuitive as the mule. And none of the horses were as eager to take trips off the ranch as the mule usually seemed to be. This was contrary to what he'd often hear others tell who owned mules. And usually it seemed, they either loved their mules, or hated them. He felt nothing less than respect and appreciation for his own beast.

When he brought the animal around to the door of the tack shed, he could sense the excitement in his manner. He knew he was going to be saddled up, and that meant he was about to embark on a journey. Sometimes he had trouble keeping still long enough to be properly saddled up, in his excitement, but Nathan had learned how to gradually calm him down with words spoken in a soft, soothing tone. He'd gotten pretty good at it, and it always worked. The mule genuinely wanted to cooperate, even when his excitement got the better of him. Nathan was always patient with him, and he responded accordingly.

His saddle rested on a five-inch diameter pine rail inside the tack shed, and even with the door completely open, it remained relatively dark inside the shed without a lantern lit. Nathan knew where everything was, so he didn't need to see much to find whatever he needed in there. He lifted the saddle off the rail with his left arm and reached for the bit and reins with his right hand.

As he carried everything toward the doorway he heard the unmistakable noise, and then he felt the fangs jab into his left arm. He immediately dropped the tack to the ground and reached for the door, looking down at where the saddle landed. A split second later he saw the rattlesnake slithering out from under it and toward the open doorway.

When the snake exited the shed and slithered out into the morning sunlight to make its escape, it caught the attention of the mule, and that was its big mistake. The mule had an aversion to such ground crawlers, and swiftly stomped the reptile into bloody shreds.

Nathan stepped from the doorway for better light to examine his left forearm. Two thin red streams emerged from tiny holes on the top of the arm, about midway up the forearm. It felt no different than having been jabbed by two long thorns, and the stinging sensation was not severe pain by any measure. Had he simply been pricked by a couple of thorns, he would just rinse the arm with cold water and wipe away the blood until dry. But this could be serious. He'd just been struck by a rattler, and the poison would soon be in his blood stream. He knew he'd have to act quickly to minimize the amount of poison getting into his system. Fortunately, it appeared that no large veins were punctured.

He didn't have his knife at hand, being dressed for a visit rather than for working around the ranch on this morning. His sheath knife was back at the house hanging from his pistol belt, and he didn't want to run back to the house for fear of getting his blood circulating rapidly through his body. But those fang holes appeared large enough to get at least some of the poison back out, so he quickly sealed his lips on the skin around the bite holes and began creating as much suction as he possibly could for as long as he could before spitting out the nasty tasting blood and poison into the tall grass by the shed. He repeated the process several times, causing the wound to bleed more and more and working to remove as much of the fluids as he could through the bite holes.

When he felt he could accomplish not much more with that activity, he decided to apply a mild tourniquet to his upper arm, if not to completely cut off the flow of blood through the arm, at least to restrict the circulation enough to slow the poison.

He grabbed a halter out of the shed and cinched up one of its straps snuggly around his arm above the elbow. His left hand soon felt numb.

The effects of the poison still hadn't hit him yet, and he knew he should get the mule saddled up for riding while he still had enough strength. He picked up the saddle blanket and saddle and positioned them on the mule's back, and got the cinches started.

The mule sensed an atmosphere of some distress, and in his anxiety was having trouble keeping still long enough for Nathan to connect the flank strap. Nathan's aggravation was compounded by his left hand, which was by this time too numb to be of much use. The memory of trying to work with numb fingers came back to him, from that day in the mountains when ropes were tight around his wrists, and his frustration increased. He was finally able calm the creature with soothing dialog combined with gently brushing the animal's barrel with his numb hand, and he eventually stood still long enough for Nathan to connect and cinch the strap, and the rest of the riding tack.

The sun felt warmer now, almost hot, and Nathan was beginning to feel the symptoms of the snakebite; dizziness, headache, blurred vision, and his left arm was starting to swell. He decided that the tourniquet probably wasn't helping anything, so he removed it.

He led the mule to a shaded area under some trees, and there he sat himself down on the ground. This rest would only be for a few minutes, he told himself, just long enough for him to regain his steadiness. After a bit he'd get himself up into the saddle. Just a brief period of rest to regain himself was all he felt he needed right now.

After resting a short while he made an attempt to climb into the saddle. But by then he was so weak and dizzy he struggled even to stand up without falling over, and he simply collapsed against the base of a tree where he closed his eyes to rest a bit longer. He was already feeling pretty rough, and sweating profusely even in the shade, and he realized there had to be more poison in his blood than he previously expected.

The hallucinations seemed to occur right away. At one point he was certain he'd seen Milton Galley, standing next to the tack shed trying to tell him something. "The wedding." He seemed to be saying. "The wedding is about to begin. You've got to get your hide over there and interrupt the proceedings. Don't be worryin' about that little rattler bite. Get yourself on over there. Emily doesn't love him, she loves *you.*"

But only a second later he opened his eyes again and the old timer was gone. The poison was playing tricks on his mind. He couldn't be sure from one moment to the next what was from the real world, and what came from his delusions. This was a nightmarish state of being that might only go away if he could fall asleep. Sleep could only be good for him at this point. Sleep it off. Rest the body. Slow down the racing heartbeat. Rest. That was what he needed right now.

His fitful slumber was interrupted by the nudging against his head, and he awoke to large mule nostrils breathing on his face. By now his headache was impossible to ignore. It occurred to him that he needed to get some help. Clearly the mule had the same sense of things, and that was why he had nudged him awake – so he could get up and do something about his condition.

But what could he do? Maybe if he got himself up to the well he could drink some fresh cool water. That would help replenish what he had lost through perspiration. If he could get himself to a doctor, then he'd have expert help. But the nearest doctor was…

He remembered the wedding. He was probably too late now to stop the marriage from happening, but the bridegroom was a doctor. The Thibault Ranch wasn't far away. He should be able to ride over there inside of twenty minutes. It appeared to be his best chance.

But after several failed attempts, he discovered that he lacked sufficient energy to climb up into the saddle. If he couldn't mount the mule, he knew he wouldn't be going very far to anywhere.

The mule understood his dilemma, and slowly lowered himself as much as he could to make it easier for his master. Seeing this gave Nathan inspiration for another try at it, and with a degree of effort was able to seat himself into the saddle. The mule then recovered to his usual stance, and the two were off on their way in the direction of the closest neighbors'.

It was hard telling how much time had elapsed since his encounter with the snake. By the position of the sun, he guessed it was early afternoon, but he wasn't in a frame of mind to refine his calculation any better than that from the back of a mule in stride. At this point it didn't seem to make much difference. He knew he would soon find someone, and he would soon have water to drink, if nothing else. There was always somebody home on the ranch.

A multitude of thoughts crowded his mind now. Everything Stewart told him in the hardware store rang contradictory to his own expectations, but if his present estimation of time proved at all close to accurate, he would be arriving after the wedding ceremony had concluded anyway, and Emily would be the married lady he'd believed her to be all of these last few months. The notion that he might have *had* a reasonable chance of changing that reality, not just once but now at least twice, and foolishly missed his opportunity each time was a difficult issue to contemplate. But it would be too late to worry about that now.

Even in his miserable state, he couldn't stop thinking about the baby boy – his own son, according to Stewart. He couldn't stop wondering about him. It was almost difficult to comprehend. But it must be true. Stewart wouldn't have any reason to invent something like that.

His thoughts about his son gave him inspiration to keep himself seated in the saddle, and to keep himself awake as best he could. For even if the snakebite was to bring him to an early grave, which currently seemed quite possible the way he was feeling, he wanted at least to have first seen his son. Soon he wouldn't be able to see much of anything, as blurry as his vision was getting.

He had a sense of direction, even though he couldn't see too well by now. It wouldn't have mattered, though, because the mule knew where he needed to go. The mule had been to the Thibault Ranch before, and he knew that the people there were acquainted with Nathan. It was the only logical place to carry his master, who was by now leaning over forward with the saddle horn pressing against his stomach. Nathan was barely holding on when the mule's hooves touched ground on the neighboring ranch, and he was barely conscious.

Emily caught the first glimpse of the distant animal that appeared to be approaching the house, before anyone else had noticed, and it wasn't clear to her initially whether the animal carried a rider or not. But she strained her eyes for a closer look, and eventually she felt certain there was somebody on the back of the animal. She held her breath. Could that someone be Nathan? Whoever it was appeared to be in a very bad way, the way he was hunched over in his saddle. As the animal approached closer, she eventually recognized it as the same beast of burden that carried the rider she met for the first time one sunny day last June, and her life had never been the same since that day. It was the same mule, and he had a rider on his back now, just like before, only this time the rider wasn't sitting tall and proud in the saddle. This time the rider appeared to be barely alive. He was barely holding on.

"Nate!!!" She screamed, soon running as fast as she could run in her wedding dress toward the approaching mule. "It's Nathan," she cried "and he's hurt!"

Everyone still present chased after her toward the approaching animal. Seeing this crowd moving toward him, the mule stopped and turned sideways, and Nathan fell unconsciously out of the saddle onto the grass covered field, lying motionless like a clump of dirt clods on the ground. The mule took a few steps back and away from where everyone suddenly gathered. He didn't move too far away; not more than twenty feet from where his master lay on the ground.

Emily dropped to her knees at Nathan's side, and inspected him for injuries. He tried to speak, mumbling something incoherently, which she didn't understand. And then he managed to point to his left arm, and she saw the fang marks on the swollen part of the arm.

"Oh my God!" She gasped. "He's been bitten by something! Something like… Oh no! Only a rattlesnake bites like that. We've got to him some water, and fast."

Stewart and Jacob picked Nathan up and carried him all the way to the house, where Mrs. Rhodes got a pail of fresh water and a wash cloth ready to cool him down with. Emily stayed close to his side, this time careful not to let him out of her sight, even for an instant. Gabriel was left momentarily in the care of one of the trusted guests, a Mrs. Redding, who'd never had any children of her own, but who could never get her fill of helping others with theirs. There were still some other guests at the ranch, and the house was turning into quite an atmosphere of urgency, with people rushing here and there, to bring this or that to the bed where Nathan was being nursed.

"He'll be all right, won't he?" Emily asked hopefully, with more than a hint of worry in her voice.

"'Course he will, Princess." Assured her father. "Seen men struck by rattlers b'fore. Mostly ever one of 'em came out of it just fine."

He looked at Stewart. They both knew a man who was killed by a rattlesnake years ago, before Emily was old enough to understand, but neither wanted to talk about that case right now. Just like Emily, they were hoping it wasn't going to be that serious for Nathan.

As hopeful as any of them wanted to be about his recovery, the reality that his condition wasn't looking good was pretty hard to ignore. Emily and Mrs. Rhodes worked diligently to cool him down with moist wash cloths, but there seemed to be no relief from his misery.

He went in and out of consciousness. At one point he thought he heard them debating about whether or not to go find Dr. Lukehorn. Emily seemed to be talking them out of it, saying something about how angry the doctor had been, and how she no longer trusted him with his "mysterious potions". She wasn't particularly eager to place Nathan's life in the hands of someone with such wicked resentment in his eyes. Dr. Lukehorn would be the *last* person she'd turn to for saving Nathan's life, she explained, and she stubbornly insisted on keeping the doctor away. Nobody challenged her on that stand.

What he'd heard was very much like a dream created in his own delusional mind, and he wasn't completely sure it wasn't just a dream. But what it implied, if indeed true, was that she hadn't gotten married. The doctor was not currently present on the ranch. Although he had suspected that a doctor might help him, this news was welcome news to Nathan. She hadn't married the doctor, and the doctor wasn't present.

It was enough to make him really want to live. Snakebite or not, he had plenty to live for now. The doctor was gone. Nathan's mind searched for clues that might convince him he'd heard correctly, and that he wasn't having a dream. It seemed so real, and then it seemed so much like a dream, it was impossible to be sure. And he couldn't see a thing but blurry shapes. But if this was real...

He was determined now. He would survive this terrible poisoning. He would keep his mind going – keep himself awake and stay alive. He would will himself well. It was all he had now; his will. But he had to survive, and live. He couldn't leave Emily now. He couldn't leave his son. He couldn't move at all, though he tried. And he couldn't see. It was going to be real tough, but he was going to live. He had plenty to live for now, and he had his will power; his determination. Emily was close to him now.

CHAPTER XIII

It was all just a memory now. The events that brought Nathan and Emily together all occurred more than half a dozen years ago, and now they both perceived the ordeals each endured then as important ingredients in the cement binding them together. Everything seemed so completely a part of destiny.

Gabriel Clayburn celebrated his sixth birthday just a few months ago. His parents couldn't get over how fast he seemed to be growing. Last summer they got him a dog to play with; a golden retriever, and he and his dog were inseparable now. They had the range of two big ranches to explore, and there was never a moment of boredom with them.

Emily and Nathan sat together in the settee on their front porch now, enjoying the gentle California breeze that carried with it the pleasant fragrances from Emily's flower garden, and they listened attentively to the singing of birds and the rustling of aspen leaves in the breeze. They watched Gabriel play with his dog out in the field. This was a relaxing Sunday afternoon in late June, seven years to the day from their first meeting, and the comfortable warm air sweeping through the open porch took their minds back to that moment.

Gabriel threw a stick as far as he could throw it, which wasn't very far, and his dog went after it to bring it back to him. As he watched him chase after it, he noticed a horse and rider in the far south end of the ranch, approaching in the direction of the house.

"Father," he pointed toward the rider he saw "are we going to have a visitor today?"

Nathan and Emily focused their attention in the direction Gabriel pointed. The rider was just far enough away that he was difficult to recognize. He was also approaching from the opposite direction of the Thibault Ranch, so it wasn't likely Jacob or Stewart. Besides, the horse was darker than any of theirs, and this rider's hat was wider than what they all preferred wearing. It took awhile for him to reach the vicinity of the house, during which time Nathan and Emily speculated quietly about who he was, and why he was here. As he came closer, Nathan was certain he'd never seen this individual before. The rider didn't look any older than about eighteen, when he was close enough to clearly see his face.

The dust kicked up by hooves had hardly vanished in the wind when the rider drew in reins and halted within twenty yards of the front of the porch. Nathan waited to see what the rider had come for before taking his right hand off of the Colt Army .44 hidden behind his back on the chair. Since that day at his camp on that mountain stream seven years ago when those two scoundrels jumped him, he always kept a loaded revolver within quick reach, just in case. You couldn't be too careful in these parts, even on your own land. But this young rider didn't seem too threatening, so Nathan took his right hand off the butt of the gun. His left arm remained around Emily, who sat close at his side.

Gabriel seemed thoroughly curious about this visitor, until his dog distracted him by barking for his attention.

The rider tipped his hat at the Clayburns. "Afternoon, sir, ma'am. I apologize for intrudin' like this, on a Sunday and all, but wudja mind if I filled my water jugs at your well? Been a warm day, this one, and I've been a long time ridin'. The mouth is pretty dry."

"No mind at all." Nathan answered. "Help yourself. Water's something we got plenty of. The well's just over there." He nodded toward the well and the young rider turned to look.

"You're welcome to water your horse, too, if you wish." Nathan offered. "Direction you're headed comes into some year-round cricks. Water's high right now with snow runoff, but that's another mile and a half. We keep a trough full of fresh water for our horses, and you're welcome to it."

"Thank you kindly." He said, and started to turn his animal in the direction of the watering trough when Emily spoke to him.

"What brings you to this part of the country?" She asked him. "You're a long ways from somewhere. I can tell by the size of that pack roll behind your saddle. You're on some kind of long journey, aren't you?"

He turned back around to face her. "Yes, ma'am. That's right. As a matter o'fact, I'm on a voyage into those Sierra Mountains." He nodded toward the hills within view of the ranch.

"You wouldn't be a gold prospector, would you?" Nathan asked him.

He nodded. "Yessir, that's what I'm goin' up into them mountains to do. I've heard some stories, but I've gotta see about it for myself. They say there was an old timer who lived alone like a hermit up in them mountains, who knew how to find as much gold as he ever wanted, whenever he ever wanted. Hard tellin' which stories to believe, and which ones are just plain fabrications, but it all caught my interest just the same. So, here I am."

"Ever prospected for gold before?"

"No sir. But I've read books."

"Books are fine," said Nathan "but there's no substitute for hard-earned experience. You'll gain that, all right, if you stay at it. No guarantees you'll ever find any, but some have. Indeed, some have done right well. Those mountains can be treacherous, and you can run into trouble. I see you got a new looking gun there on your belt. One of those cartridge-firing Peacemakers, is it?"

"Sure is. Colt's forty-five. I paid eighteen American dollars for it. Had to pay a little extra, just to get one. Most of 'em go to the Army."

"Well, it's a wise investment. A man needs a good shooter where you're headed. I've spent some time myself in those mountains. I know them well. The California Gold Rush was a whole quarter of a century ago and more, but prospectors still find nuggets on occasion."

The young rider was clearly intrigued by Nathan's talk of the Sierras, and finding gold. There was a sense he'd liked to have stayed awhile and discussed more of the subject, but the afternoon was wearing on, and he knew he still had a long ride ahead of him before making camp. He'd planned on just watering up and then getting along on his voyage. Understanding all of this, Emily invited him to stay for supper. A man on a voyage must get awfully hungry, she reckoned.

"She's a fine cook, my wife is." Nathan added. "And if you stay for supper, I can draw you a map how to find a particular crick you might try panning. Might pick up some decent nuggets there. Some prospectors I know did mighty well on that crick. But I've also got some good bear stories to tell."

"What about Indians? There a lot of Indians up there?" He asked.

"Thing to remember about most kinds of Indians around here is they usually see you before you see them, and that's if they want you to see them. You're not likely to have trouble with them, so long as you keep to yourself. But you always want to be on your guard. Let your guard down one time, and that'll be the time you'll regret it. All kinds of people travel through those mountains, for all kinds of reasons, and not all of 'em are good people. So it's wise to always have that shooter ready where you can get to it in a hurry, just in case."

The young rider was grateful to share supper with the Clayburns, and he learned everything he could from Nathan in the duration of his short visit, and then he continued on his prospector's voyage up into the Sierra Nevada Mountains.

Some might not understand what draws a man to the wild places with little more than a horse, some basic provisions, a gun, a gold pan, and a dream, but Nathan understood it. He was never very good at explaining it, perhaps, but he understood it perfectly.

The End

ABOUT THE AUTHOR

James Ballou is an avid reader of American history and frontier life. His own writing ranges from imaginative fiction in several different genres to educational nonfiction, and more than two dozen of his articles have appeared in various wilderness magazines. *The Prospector's Voyage* is his first published novel.

1151497

Made in the USA